Twins of Prey III

~

Ascension

W.C. Hoffman

ISBN: 1499645031
ISBN-13: 978-1499645033

DEDICATION

For my wife, Alicia,
Who responded "Maybe if you're lucky," when I asked her to marry me.
It turns out, I truly am the lucky one.

ACKNOWLEDGMENTS

The entire Twins of Prey series would never have become what it is today without the inspiration and guidance of many other authors who have helped me find my way in the world of publishing. I hope you read their books and enjoy their talents as much as I have.

I would like to thank the following authors:

Gary Paulsen, Tim Moon, Sean Platt, David Wright, Johnny B. Truant, Sarah Mack, Simon Whistler, Jennifer Fisch-Ferguson, Bryan Cohen, Jim Kukral, Ashley Jeffers, Darren Wearmouth, Carl Sinclair, Ken Magee, and Wayne Stinne

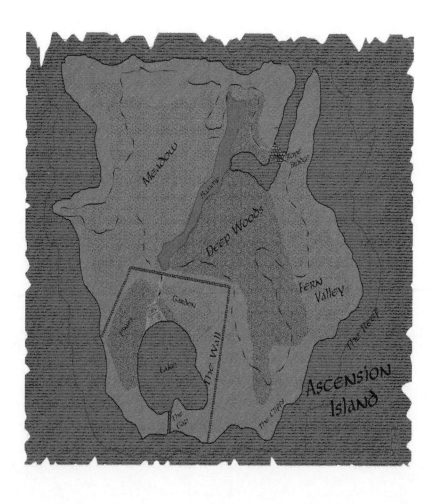

1 TURBLANCE

The hum of the single prop engine drowned out every sound in the small cockpit as twin brothers Tomek and Drake sat in the back bucket seats, uncomfortably handcuffed together while looking out the windows at the glistening, Lake Michigan water below them. The small aircraft seemed to dart through the sparse cloud cover while continually bouncing up and down amongst the invisible air pockets that listed the mechanical bird up and down, much like a raft upon a raging, white river.

Drake, with his head pressed against the window, seemed to be enjoying the ride and sights from above much more than his identical, twin counterpart who stayed in place with his own head buried in his lap and both eyes tightly closed.

"What's a matter, Tomek?" their older sister, Annette, asked with a giggle, knowing he could hear her through the headphones the three of them adorned prior to taking off.

"Birds—birds are meant to fly, not us," he answered. "This thing only has one engine and, if it dies, how far can you—we—glide?" Tomek asked, worried about the stability of the plane in relation to his fate.

"All the way to the crash site, I imagine," his sister responded while pushing the yoke straight down, causing the aircraft to aggressively nosedive in a successful attempt to scare him even more.

Not wanting to give her the satisfaction of knowing his true level of terror, he ignored the fact that his stomach was now in his throat and placed his head back into his lap while mumbling, "Good one."

After taking off from her marina hangar on Lake Huron near the small town of Oscoda, the float plane took very little time passing over the former, local Air Force base en route to their destination. She pointed the prop west and quickly reached the shore of the neighboring Great Lake on the opposite side of Michigan's northern Lower Peninsula. At that point, she continued on a course due northwest until land could not be seen in any direction.

"What is the plan, exactly?" Drake asked.

"You will see shortly," she answered, not giving him any details.

"I am guessing we're escaping to Canada," Tomek added, his head back in his lap.

Drake fought the sleep that was clawing at his soul. They had all been awake for what seemed like days. With the blood of the Angels still fresh on their hands, the twins were clueless as to what their sister had planned for them.

Trooper Common and Sheriff Henderson had driven almost straight to the marina after leaving the death scene at Lucky Trail. After making a quick stop to drop Trooper Common off at Henderson's house to process the crime scene, from that point on it was just Tomek, Drake, and Annette. They were together again, alone as a family for the first time since she had tried to drown them in Uncle's underground cabin.

"How did you learn to fly?" Tomek asked.

"This is my first time," she answered, causing them both to smirk. It was as if they had spent their whole lives together and this was just another, non-stop moment of sibling humor.

"Hilarious," Tomek said while rolling his eyes.

"Seriously, what the hell is going on?" Drake asked again.

Henderson replied by saying, "You are being detained, pending a complete investigation into the murder of one hundred and seventy-six juvenile souls."

"We didn't kill them!" Tomek yelled while sitting up and jerking his hand forward, which yanked Drake's in return due to the shared handcuff.

"I know," said their sister, the Sheriff, as she again pushed the yoke down while operating the flaps to drop them out of the cloud cover.

With the float plane now being through the blinding whiteness and only eighty feet above the water's surface, the twins could look ahead through the windshield and see the land mass a few miles away.

"What do you mean you know we didn't kill them?" Drake asked.

"I know you didn't kill those boys at Lucky Trail," Annette responded.

"Yea, and how is that?" Tomek wondered, as if he was challenging what she knew to be the truth.

"The video," she said.

"Like, the security camera footage?" Drake asked.

"No, not that video, but we will be watching all that. Father Niko sent a tape to the Sheriff's department and news channels as well as letters to all the newspapers. He confessed his sins, which in return absolved yours. That is why we showed up there in the first place. I am sure it is a media circus right now, and that's why I got you out of there as quick as possible. I figured you were not feeling up to doing news interviews as the kids who survived." Annette was joking about the interviews, but she knew it was the truth.

"What about the angels?" Tomek asked in a tone that sounded as if he was almost bragging.

"He sent them to kill me, you stopped them. So as far as I am concerned, they took each other out. No one needs to know the truth about them, or you." Sheriff Henderson explained to her brothers that she was once again covering up murders that they had committed in order to protect them. It was becoming clearer every moment that she was someone they could truly

3

trust.

Silence fell upon the cockpit as the boys both slouched back into their chairs and pondered why a person who they had tried to kill would again help them. Either way, they were lucky to be alive, and both felt that sitting in that small cockpit handcuffed to each other was much better than being handcuffed to each other in a jail cell.

The plane bobbed up and down as it continued to descend while staying on course, heading straight for the massive, rock-walled island that lay before them. As they flew closer, the boys both inched up to the edge of their red leather seats to obtain a better view.

Not only noticing the obvious island formation that seemed to float upon the surface, the color of the water itself was noticeably different here as well. It transitioned from a deep blue to an emerald green, with pockets of dark amber just below the surface.

"Why does the water look like that?" Drake asked his sister.

"It's an optical illusion," she explained. "You see, the island is surrounded by a freshwater barrier reef, and the color difference is just because of the drastic depth changes. No boats can get to this island because of the reef. Even smaller vessels run aground or get tossed in the heavy, rolling wave action that the reef produces. Coming to or leaving this island in any form of a boat is a death trap. Doing so will lead to a capsized, destroyed vessel for sure and usually worse. The occupants of which will hopefully drown before being violently tossed against the rocks by the shoreline breakers and beaten to death thanks to the unforgiving, sharp edges. In all honesty, it is pretty nasty down there."

From their sky-high vantage point, what she was telling them matched the clear picture that was laid out below them. The rocky and shallow reef seemed to be about one hundred yards wide and completely encased the island. Separating the edge of the reef and the island was a three-quarter island section of dark blue water with unexplainable large waves that constantly crashed into the black rock walls.

The pure beauty of this oasis in the middle of Lake Michigan was almost indescribable. The only land mass for miles around, it was obvious that for some reason the glacial impacts of millennia ago had missed this spot as they carved out the current, Great Lakes lake bed. Looking at the wall of rock, a large, roughly circular section appeared to be missing, leaving an opening that might just be big enough for the float plane to fit through if it had been flown by an experienced pilot.

Getting closer and closer to the hole in the rock wall, it was clear that the plane's wingspan would indeed fit through it. If Annette had lined up her approach correctly, that was. However, one shift in the wind or banking too much would result in the plane slamming directly against the dark, black, ironclad rock wall. In which case, again, the forceful impact would kill the lucky ones, and the survivors would fall to their demise amongst the waves and rocks below.

As the plane neared its final lineup, it dawned on Drake exactly what his older sister was about to attempt.

"What in the hell are you doing?" he asked, questioning his sister's sanity.

"What does it look like? Now, shut the hell up and be quiet. This is not the easiest thing in the world to do. So I have been told."

"What? I hope you are joking." Tomek voiced his concern.

"Hold on tight," she yelled as the plane entered the tunnel and all went black. The dark-rock and moss-outlined island mountainside hole swallowed them as if they had entered a different dimension.

Drake was unsure if it was the darkness of the tunnel they had just flown into that blinded him or if he had just clinched his eyes shut so hard in anticipation for the crashing impact. The vibrations of the spinning propeller and roaring engine reverberated off the walls and shook the plane like it suddenly had been flying through a warzone with exploding anti-aircraft munitions all around them.

Tomek kept his eyes open, and, with only the glow of the instrument panel visible in the dark, fear took over each sense in his body. Suddenly, there in the dark, his eyes rolled back into his head and all was quiet. The roaring sound of the engine as his sister piloted the plane became silent, and the only audible thing he could sense coming through the headphones was the rapid beating of his own heart.

Thumpa, thump, thumpa, thump…

Feeling his body lose control and let go, Tomek began slumping into the back deepness of his seat. Just prior to losing all consciousness and blacking out from the gravity of the situation, he sprang awake as they exited the tunnel into a burst of light, causing each one of his senses to thunder back to life with a vengeance.

Exiting the tunnel and leaving the vast rock wall behind them, they looked down upon what appeared to be a miniature paradise. A crystal-clear, emerald bay with no waves gave way to a white, sandy beach that reminded them both of the Caribbean sands they read about in the books that Uncle had in the underground cabin.

Aggressively dropping altitude yet again, the boys felt their stomachs slam into what felt like the top of their throats.

"Sorry about that," Henderson said. "It's the only way to get this thing down and land in the bay. That's why we had to use the tunnel up there. No way to come over the top and land safely. Too high of an angle once you clear the rock."

Skimming the aircraft just over the surface of the water, she slowly leveled down the throttle until the back of the landing floats began to drag along the surface of the pristine lake, slowing them down and lurching them forward as the plane became totally reliant on the buoyancy of both sets of floats. Turning the plane back to the south with the tail rudder, she taxied up to the beach, throttled down, and killed the engine as the floats dragged against the sand, bringing the aircraft to a halt.

"What is this place?" Tomek asked.

"Ascension Island," she answered, waving her hand outward and up, almost like she was a travel agent showing off the property before them.

"And what is Ascension Island?" Drake joined in on the conversation.

"Well, brothers, is it not obvious?" she asked, receiving dumbfounded looks and shoulder shrugs from both of her younger siblings.

"This—this is Ascension Island," she said again, making the same travel-agent-displaying hand and arm movement as before.

"Okay, and what is Ascension Island?" Drake again asked, mimicking her hand gesture and tone of voice, which made Tomek smile for a few seconds before he remembered that he felt sick to his stomach.

Annette looked back at them as she tossed a set of handcuff keys into their laps and said, "It's your new home."

2 BEACH

Removing the shared handcuffs from their wrists, each twin rubbed the skin where the metal had pressed against it in an effort to lessen the pain caused by the Smith & Wesson brand, brushed nickel, metallic cuffs.

The beach was composed of pristine white sand and only a few, lone piles of driftwood and seaweed rested along its shoreline. Both twins were impressed with its clean appearance and overall beauty. Stepping out of the cockpit and atop of the float, Tomek was uneasy on his feet. The combination of the float's slippery surface matched with the bobbing action of it still being half in the water made his legs weakly give out. Almost falling in the water, he was able to grab the wing support and steady himself before meeting the cold water for a swim.

"What is this place?" Drake asked as he bent down and picked up a handful of the dry, white sand. Running the sand through his fingers, the quality and grit of it surprised him. It was different than the beaches of their river, in color, clarity, and grit.

"This is Ascension Island," she again said.

"Yea, you mentioned that," Tomek reminded her, rolling his eyes.

"It is ours. Well, it is yours, I mean." Annette continued explaining, "This entire island belonged to the Henderson Lumber Company. Although they never did actually harvest any lumber from it, thanks to the Kirtland's warblers using it as a nesting location. Our grandfather bought it back in the 1940s and then used it as a vacation spot. They imported a bunch of exotic wildlife, and the island was their own hunting and game preserve."

"So, our family is rich?" Drake asked.

"Was rich," Henderson replied.

"So, you are just going to leave us out here? On a stranded island in the middle of Lake Michigan, all alone?" Tomek asked.

"Yep, that's the idea."

Tomek threw his hands up in the air and began walking towards her. His demeanor made her nervous, causing her right hand to find its way atop of the pistol on her hip.

"That is—that is—that is the nicest thing anyone has ever done for us," Tomek said as he closed the distance to her, embracing his sister in a big, bear-like hug that lifted her off her feet slightly as he leaned back.

A smile found its way upon her face.

"So, you are happy?" she asked.

"Yes, we are," Drake said, echoing his twin brother's sentiment with a smile. "But what is here on this island?" Drake was already thinking about the logistics of their survival.

"And what the hell is a Kirtland's warbler?" Tomek added.

"It's an endangered species of bird and the only reason the island is protected. No one from the outside world is allowed to come here in order to let the birds repopulate in the jack pines and hardwoods on the island. This place has everything you will need and more. I will give you a map later, but for now look around you," she said while spinning around, taking in the views.

"Seventy-six hundred acres of wild are all yours. Full of deer, turkey, hogs, and all the weird stuff they imported here over the years."

"Weird stuff?" Tomek asked.

"Yea, they have impala and kudu, and at one time there was a hippo in this very lake. Or at least our Grandfather claimed there was," Henderson said.

"A hippo?" Drake was immediately skeptical.

"Sorry, 'hippo' is short for 'hippopotamus,' " she replied, smirking.

"Oh, that's what you meant by 'hippo,' huh?" Drake was now laying on the sarcasm pretty thick in response as the three of them all seemed to enjoy the barbing tone of the conversation.

"Well, I never saw it, but Grandpa said at one time, years ago, they bought one from a zoo that was closing and brought it out here. But I'm guessing they either killed it or it died during the winter."

"What is the deal with this beach and lake?" Drake continued asking questions.

"Yea. Why didn't you just land outside the island instead of flying through that freaking hole?" Tomek jumped in on the information probe of his sister.

Sitting down on the soft sand, she just looked at them. Taking a handful of it up in her fist she squeezed it, watching it escape from between her fingers as it fell back down to the beach top.

"See this?" she said.

"Yes, it's sand," Tomek answered.

"When we circled the island, did you see any of it anywhere else?" she asked.

The twins both shook their heads in a 'no' fashion but felt it was somewhat of an unfair question being that they were not exactly on the lookout for sand-covered beaches at the time.

"Exactly," Henderson said, putting the rest of the sand down as she stood up. "There is none, only rock. That is why this island was the perfect game preserve. The entire edge is a straight drop-off onto the rocks below. No fences needed, no trespassers, and no chance for escape. Anything, or anyone, that jumps off the edge dies upon impact or drowns."

"So, what you're saying is this is the perfect prison?" Drake asked, questioning his sister's motives.

"It would be for anyone—anyone other than people like you. For people like you—" Henderson said prior to being interrupted by Tomek.

"People like us? What the hell does that mean?"

"You know exactly what that means," his older sister replied, shutting down his bravado attempt at trying to stir something up.

"Yea, I guess you're right. People like us," Tomek said, smiling and looking at Drake while he shrugged his shoulders.

"This inland lake is stocked with all the fish you could dream of. It is spring fed and always nice and cold in the summer," she said, confirming the temperature of the water by dipping her hand in it.

"The only way on or off the island is by float plane. Boats can't come here, and we are too far off of either the Lower Peninsula or the Upper for a helicopter to fly here. And since pilots don't know about the gap—and if they did, most wouldn't shoot the gap like we did—you will be safe here. Alone to hunt, alone to fish, alone to garden, alone to live, and alone to survive." Henderson's words made both of the twins instantly excited for their new life here on Ascension Island.

"Still, though, why shoot the gap at all?" Drake asked.

"It is a flight and altitude issue. This island is made almost completely of iron ore. That's why all the rocks are black. Which is the entire reason our family originally bought it. Back then, just as much as now, the iron ore mining industry was very profitable. Our Henderson Company had their fingers in everything. Lumber, rail, and mining were by far the biggest here in Michigan."

"Thanks for the history lesson, but what in the hell does that have to do with shooting the gap?" Tomek asked again.

"The iron ore here is mostly magnetite, which messes with the instruments and dials on the plane," Henderson said. "Dropping in here over the cliff and into this bowl-shaped canyon from the top means you have to do multiple circles while dropping altitude and avoiding the large pieces of rock that jut out from the wall on all sides. Doing so without instruments is suicide. Even more so than shooting the gap." Henderson then looked at her brothers, waiting for their response in order to confirm that they were satisfied with her answer.

"So, do you have to shoot the gap to leave as well?" Drake asked.

"No, thank God," she replied. "Climbing out is easy, and gaining enough altitude to clear the rocks is not an issue."

"I will fly over and drop supplies every two weeks or so, If you need me to land and stop, there is a flagpole on the peak of the cliff. Just raise the flag, and I will know something is wrong. If I see the flag, I shoot the gap and land. That is my plan so far. What do you guys think?" their sister asked, in order to make them feel as if they actually had a choice in the matter. Which, of course, they did not.

However, it was not the boys that answered her. The piercingly loud and high-pitched bugle of a bull elk cut through the air, causing them all to look up into the mountain-like, wooded, hillside range.

"I think we are going to like it here," Tomek said.

"I think so too," Drake agreed.

3 SAFE

"Time to start hunting," Tomek said as he looked at his siblings, hoping they were ready to go chase down the nearby, bugling elk as well.

Drake agreed, but, as he was prone to do, he looked at the situation more realistically. "What are you going to do, Tomek? Beat the damn thing's head in with a beach rock?"

"If only we had bows," Tomek replied sarcastically, looking at Annette.

"Plenty of elk here, little brother. Plenty of deer and all the weird stuff, too. You can hunt later, but for now let's get you settled in the cabin," Henderson said, ending their fun.

"Cabin?" Tomek asked.

"Yea, just up this trail. It will need some work, as it has been years since anyone has been here. But you guys will have nothing but time, and I am sure it will suit you just fine." She smiled while passing the boys as they left the beach area on the most obvious of trails that lead from the beach sand up and into the woodland area.

After leaving the beach area, it was only a short walk of about forty yards until they found themselves in a wood lot full of tall, mature, hardwood trees. The mature oak and hickory giants provided both adequate shade and cover for the cabin, which sat nestled into a small opening. Their mass of acorns lay upon the ground, and, with the bumper crop under their feet, it was like walking on Mother Nature's marbles.

Looking at the small, rectangular cabin that stood before them with its lime green siding and screened-off entry porch, both boys were surprised at the relatively good condition of the structure. The building had served as the base camp for all the hunting operations on the island during its prime run as a vacation spot for the Henderson family. It was small, simple, and perfect for their needs. Stepping up on the cement stairs, they walked inside the small, screened-in porch area and then through the front door. The three of them stood in a small dining room, with the far wall serving as the kitchen.

The walls were not lined with white birch bark as their original underground cabin that they shared with Uncle was, but the wood paneling on the walls still provided a rustic sense of décor. The poorly carpeted and dusty wood floors creaked as they walked across the room, much like the floorboards at Old Man Hawkins' now-burnt-down store. Their new home shared many of the characteristics of their previous two, and they both felt comfortable as they began digging into the cabin a little deeper.

Against the kitchen wall was an old, white, porcelain, farm-style sink, an icebox, and even an old, brick-style oven that resembled the same one the pizzeria in Pine Run used to make their pepperoni pies. Tomek walked over to the sink, lifted the faucet handle up, and was surprised to find that the running water was still working.

"You have running water, but don't drink it," their sister warned.

"Poisoned?" Tomek asked.

"No, it just tastes like shit," she replied, laughing. "There is an artesian well just up the beach that feeds into the lake. Use that for drinking water by filling up these large, orange coolers," Henderson said while pointing out the five-gallon plastic jugs that looked like they belonged on the sideline of a high school, Friday night football game.

Turning the water on and then off again rapidly as if it was some kind of a magic trick, Tomek looked at the other two and remarked, "I have to be honest, this is a lot nicer than our old hole in the ground."

Looking around at their surroundings, both Annette and Drake nodded their heads in agreement.

"I haven't been here in a long time. Our dad only brought me here a couple of times, but I remember it fondly. My grandmother…" She paused, looking at her brothers. "Our grandmother used to sit right here. They always played cards while smoking their cigarettes and laughing. Leaving this island without learning how to play euchre, cribbage, or rummy was not an option."

Evidence of those years gone by was still present on the table. A crystal glass candy bowl remained in the middle of the table, holding various decks of game-worn playing cards, their boxes held together with dry, rotted rubber bands. Also taking up residence in the bowl were multiple pens and a small pad of paper that still held the score to every game of Michigan-style rummy that had been played in years long gone by.

Continuing through the kitchen area was a small living room with a single bedroom attached off of it to the north. A loveseat-style couch, not much bigger than a rocking chair, mostly filled the available space. It was clear that the living room was in need of structural work as the ceiling was low enough that the boys' heads almost touched it as they entered. A fireplace with its mortared brick wall on the west end of the house would be more than enough to heat the tiny home. The boys were liking their new home more and more with each minute they spent inside, and, for one of the first times, Annette Henderson actually saw a true, heartfelt smile on the faces of her brothers.

Knickknacks adorned the nicotine-stained walls everywhere they looked, and, while the interior design was lacking a modern touch, these things meant nothing to the twins. They had no problem cleaning and changing it, and they would soon make it their own.

Drake walked up to an oil painting hung above the fireplace.

"Who is that?" he asked, pointing out the female pictured standing and holding a cross.

"St. Helen," Annette said.

"Is she someone special?" Drake asked.

15

"Well, kind of. Apparently, she claims to have found the original cross that Jesus was crucified on. But that stuff is all just legend. It is also the name of the hometown of a lot of our original family. That is about all I know, and that picture has always been there."

With both boys in the bedroom, again continuing their tour, Annette smiled to herself as she continued to watch them pass by a very important door. As far as the current contents of the small room behind said door, she was unsure, but she knew exactly what it was used for in the past.

"Hey, guys. Come in here," she said, standing with her back up against the butcher-block countertop near the sink.

As the twins stepped into the room, she pointed over to a door that was just to the right of the main entrance. They both had walked past it upon originally entering the cabin.

"What is in there?" Drake asked.

"Go look," she answered with a devilish grin.

Tomek reached down, turned the handle, and forced the door open inward. Stepping inside the small room, they noticed multiple, dust-lined shelves of canned food rations and military surplus MREs.

"MREs?" Tomek said while holding up the non-descript, olive-drab and green package.

"Meals Ready to Eat," Annette said.

"You seriously think we lived our entire lives in the woods with Uncle, a former United States Marine Corps survival instructor, and don't know what an MRE is?" Tomek said while rolling his eyes. "I know dammed well what they are. I just wondered why they are here." Tomek finished making his sarcastic point.

"My guess is for when the hunting is slow?" Annette suggested.

"Either way, they will help us. Let's just hope that after-five-stay-alive does not come into play here," Drake said, looking forward to the future meals which he actually had an odd fondness for.

"Anything else in there?" Annette asked, peeking into the small room from the sink area.

Tomek and Drake worked their way around the room, spinning each can of food around to check the contents, and were then delighted to see a large, chest-high, green, metallic gun safe standing in the corner.

"Oh, baby, please be unlocked," Tomek pleaded as he reached for the handle.

"I don't give a damn if it is. We are busting that bitch open," Drake replied.

Tomek grabbed the golden, brass-colored handle and attempted to turn it both right and left unsuccessfully. The shortness of the handle's travel made a loud click as it bottomed out against the engaged lock. A feeling of disappointment fell upon him and his brother both.

"Nothing is ever easy, is it?" Tomek said, shrugging his shoulders, shaking his head, looking up at the sky, and laughing off the frustration, showing a new-found composure that surprised both of his fellow siblings.

"Nine, twenty-two, seven," Annette said.

"Huh?" Tomek asked, looking at her, wondering what she meant.

"Nine, twenty-two, seven," she repeated.

"Huh?" Tomek still was clueless and asked again.

"Nine, twenty-two, sev—" Annette this time was interrupted by Drake.

Drake scolded his twin as he shoved him out of the way. "It is the code, you dumbass."

"Not only is it the code, it is your birthday," Annette told them, which caused both twins to stop and think. They never really had celebrated their birthday before. The combination of not knowing it along with the fact that Uncle never made a big deal about it made it seem trivial.

Drake began spinning the dial and entering the numbers as Annette explained to him how to use the spin-dial lock. With the seven being entered, he reached down, grabbed the handle, and pulled it to the right. The arm moved as the heavy, clunking sound of the internal locking mechanism gave way. Drake stepped back, making room for the large, safe door to swing out as he pulled it open.

Upon seeing the contents, he and Tomek both looked back to their sister and smiled.

"Did you know?" Drake asked.

"No, but I had an idea," she replied as the three of them stood there, looking into the safe.

The three siblings then began pulling out the contents, one by one.

4 BOAT

The large yacht buoyed up and down along the small waves of Lake Michigan as it motored its way out from the peaceful shallows of the South Haven Harbor. The multi-million-dollar vessel had every amenity one could imagine and truly was a luxury play toy for the rich.

This play toy belonged to none other than Garran Barr, one of the wealthiest and most powerful men in Michigan. Most of Michigan's big money had historically revolved around the lumber and automotive industries; however, the Barr family was certainly the exception. Having owned insurance agencies for most of his life, Barr had become the go-to provider for the biggest companies in the state. His entire business empire was now run by independent agents who paid him royalties in perpetuity. This allowed Barr to retire at a relatively young age.

The only thing he enjoyed more than living this lifestyle was showing it off to others, and this is exactly what his boat, *Full Coverage*—appropriately named for an insurance tycoon—was for. The 169-foot vessel was more than just a toy; it was a status symbol for the Barr family. The boat housed multiple bedrooms, a full galley kitchen, entertainment areas, a hot tub, and even a helipad that held a small, fully camouflaged, six-seat, Augusta 109 helicopter. It was not the maiden voyage for Barr on the *Full Coverage*, but it may have been his most important. Joining him on this adventure were four of his lifelong buddies and the deckhand that he had hired in town just prior to leaving the port.

Three of his guests included his longtime buddies, Greggor, Ricardo, and Sven. The three of them were better known as the Stratton brothers, each of them with varying personalities and physical attributes. Their differences aside, they were wealthy in their own right, thanks to a large chain of ice cream and dessert stores their father, Roberto Stratton, had started back in the early 1960s. Their association with the Barr family was deeply rooted as Roberto Stratton had been lifelong friends with Garran's father, a man everyone just called Tip. Garran might as well have been the fourth Stratton brother, and they all treated him as such.

Rounding out the group of entitled lackeys was Garran's son Anthony. Tony, as he preferred to be called, while being just seventeen, was enjoying his first adventure as an official member of the guys' group. For many years, he had longed to join his father and the Stratton brothers on one of their many guys-only trips, and he was very happy that the opportunity had finally presented itself.

Because the boat was one hundred and seventy feet long an operating crew was needed and on this trip that position was filled by a middle-aged man the brothers and Barr referred to as Archer. Grayson Archer had been picked up in town by Barr and offered a job on the *Full Coverage*, thanks to a simple, chance conversation the two had. Barr had stopped into the local supply store, where Archer was simply hanging out. Barr had asked an employee a simple question in regards to tying lifelines on the deck, and Archer interrupted their conversation to answer the question.

From that moment, Barr and Archer hit it off, and he was hired on the spot. Unknown to Barr, he had actually made a good choice. The man he had just brought on board on a whim had years of experience with all sizes of boats and knew this area of the Great Lakes very well. Aside from his knowledge, Archer was also big, strong, and well-built for a man in his late fifties. His outgoing personality and go-getter attitude made him a good fit on the *Full Coverage*.

With everyone hanging in the forward lounge area where Barr piloted the yacht from, the group began partaking in their particular, favorite form of mixed drinks or beer, and the mood on the boat was light and relaxed.

"Hey, Archer, toss me another beer," Sven said as he shot his first empty bottle towards the trash can in the corner of the room like a basketball, only to miss the goal, resulting in the amber, glass bottle flying out the window and into the water.

"Hey, man, come on. Have a little more respect for Mother Nature," his brother, Greggor, said as he scolded him.

"Yea, fill those empties up with water first, then toss them, so they sink. Have some decency," Ricardo added as the group all laughed about Sven's supposed, accidental littering.

"Nice one," Barr said "You guys really are the biggest pricks in the world, huh?"

"We may not be the biggest pricks in the world, but I bet we got the biggest pricks in the world," Sven boasted as he stood up and began zipping down the fly to his pants.

"Oh, dear God, sit your ass down. My child is on the boat," Barr said, laughing and pointing to Tony.

"Time for the boy to know the truth," Greggor said, laughing as he placed his hands atop his head, full of salt and pepper grey hair, and twirled his hips around as if he was dancing a hula.

"Uh, no, thanks," replied Tony as he rolled his eyes and laughed at the childish actions of the older men. "And to think all these years I was jealous that I didn't get to go on these trips with you guys."

"Yea, straighten up, or you will get tossed out like Elliot," Greggor warned the youngest passenger in a joking manner.

"Elliot?" Tony asked.

The Stratton brothers and Barr all looked at each other long enough for it to be awkward until Ricardo spoke up. "He is not on this trip since all he did was bitch about us not cooking his ass breakfast."

"Imagine that, huh," Sven butted in. "We take him hunting, on our land, and he is griping about us not providing him with breakfast."

"Elliot was a—I mean, *is* a good guy. But let's just say we expect more out of you, Archer. Elliot did set the bar pretty high. Damn guy was—*is* the best archer we ever brought out here. Anything within a hundred yards or so was in range for him. Shame he couldn't make it on this trip," Barr said, ending the discussion regarding their former hunting partner, Elliot, while looking at the guys and trying to hold back a sinister smile that even his son Tony picked up on.

Archer went behind the bar and returned with his hands full of drinks and beers for the group. He had already become the honorary bartender for the trip. Not something that was in the limited job description he was given back in town, but in all honesty he didn't mind too much as it was something he enjoyed, anyhow.

"So, I noticed you guys don't have much for fishing gear on the boat. What is this great, outdoors adventure you were bragging up back at the docks all about?" Archer asked.

"Oh, it will be an adventure all right," Barr said as he set the course on the yacht's GPS for an automatic heading, letting the autopilot continue on driving them. Now that they were free of the shallow water, obstacles such as the inland lighthouses had become nothing more than specks upon the horizon, and Barr joined the group in the consumption of an impressive amount of booze.

"You mentioned that this adventure will be like none other. What exactly are we doing?" Archer pressed on with his questions as the group migrated back to the bar for another round of drinks.

"Hunting, we are going hunting," Greggor said.

"Sweet. I love hunting. It sounds great. But where?" Archer asked.

"Where is not important," Barr began explaining "What—now, that is what is important."

"Okay, *what* are we going hunting for?" Tony chimed in as he took a sip from his beer, still feeling a little nervous about drinking underage in front of his dad.

"The wildest of beasts," Barr said triumphantly as he raised his glass into the air and smiled as the Stratton brothers all did the same in unison.

"Wild beasts, huh? Well, this is Michigan, so did you guys get some special permit to hunt wolves or something?" Archer asked.

Reaching under the back side of the handcrafted wooden bar, Sven pulled out a wireless remote control and looked at Barr. "Should we show them?" he asked.

"By all means," Barr replied as Sven clicked the single button on the device while pointing it at the back wall. As if the remote was a magic wand, panels on the walls began to move to the sides, giving way to the largest, flat screen television that Archer had ever seen in person, let alone on a boat.

The image on the screen was clearly that of a satellite map, showing most of Northern Michigan, with a yellow dot indicating their current position hundreds of nautical miles away. It was easy to see that at this point they had steamed miles offshore and were now well on their way towards Wisconsin. The only thing between them and the Badger State was a medium-sized speck of green in the middle of the water.

"I present to you our own island, my new friend," Barr said, waving his hand across the screen and stopping at the speck to point it out while spilling a bit of his drink.

As Archer walked closer to the wall-sized, television screen map to get a better look, he said, "Never heard of it or seen it on the navigational maps or charts before."

"That's because it doesn't exist, to the public, anyway," Ricardo said.

"What do you mean 'doesn't exist'?" Tony asked, confused on the statement.

"Well, until satellite images began going public, no one but our families knew much about the island. You see, our dad and your Grandpa Tip, had a mutual friend in a guy named Jack E. Henderson. The three of them owned this island and used it as their own, private hunting ranch. And being men of means, they all—shall we say—influenced those in the correct positions to keep their private getaway just that: private. They made up some bullshit story about an endangered bird or something, and after that they had their own, private ranch. Only it is more than just a simple, island hunting ranch," Ricardo professed with alcohol-infused, slurred speech, as if he was now teaching a history class while riding the buzz of his whiskey.

"More than just a ranch?" Archer asked.

"Ever shoot an impala?" Sven answered Archer's question with a question of his own.

"No, I can't say that I have, being that I have never been to Africa," Archer said, chuckling at the absurdity of the question.

"Ever shoot a rhino?" Greggor asked.

Before Archer could answer, the third Stratton brother chimed in.

"Ever kill a lion?" Ricardo quipped from behind the bar as he switched bottles and poured himself a large bourbon this time.

"Ever get chased by a tiger?" Barr asked, joining in on the fun.

Archer just looked at all of them, figuring the liquor had gone to their brains, and answered, "No, no, and hell no."

"Lions, tigers, and bears, huh?" Tony asked. "Where are we going, the Land of Oz?"

Barr lifted up his drink again in a toasting fashion while placing his arm around his son and pulling his heir in tight so their rib cages touched and announced, "No, son, not Oz. There will be no Emerald City on this trip."

"I was kidding, dad." The eye-rolls continued.

"My son, soon you will see what you have longed for all these years. Soon, we—no—I will welcome you to our island, Ascension Island," Barr pronounced as if he expected applause from a larger audience than the one he had in front of him.

But there was no applause, just drunken chatter as the three Stratton men raised their drinks and joined him cheering "Ascension Island."

"Now, drink up and enjoy the night. We have a long way to go, and the damn boat drives itself," the eldest of the Stratton brothers, Greggor, said as he turned the radio on and cracked open a fresh beer, handing it to the youngest Barr on the boat, Tony.

"Crank up this song. I love this fucking song," Ricardo yelled.

"And she is climbing the stairway to Heaven," Archer sang along, raising his beer in the air as a toast.

"What a great song," Sven yelled, raising his drink as well while sharing a grin with his two brothers and Garran.

Both Archer and Tony noticed the grins and knew they were being left out on some form of inside joke; but neither questioned the group, and both went back to enjoying their libations.

Archer, with drink in hand, looked around the room and took in all that was in front of him. Good food, good drinks, a great boat, and an adventure with a group of new friends. He thought to himself that he must be the luckiest guy in the world, unaware that luck had nothing to do with it. He soon would understand that the most dangerous game on Ascension Island was not imported from Africa.

5 BOWS

With the green, fire rated safe door fully open, the boys marveled at the simplicity of the weaponry inside. High-powered assault weapons, hunting rifles, and perhaps jewels or gold would have been expected to have been stored in a safe of this caliber. Yet there was none of those things inside the protected vault. The black interior shelves held only stacks and stacks of what seemed to be hand-crafted wooden arrows, each ending with a razor-sharp, metallic broadhead. They had seen these heads for sale in Old Man Hawkins' store and knew that they were a vast improvement upon the stone ones they would have ended up making themselves.

Below the arrows, the majority of the safe was empty, other than two, wooden bows and a single, leather-bound journal that appeared mostly empty but did have a small amount of what looked like names written in it along with a roughly sketched map of the island and its trail system.

"Looks like some guy named Elliot was the last visitor here," Drake said.

"Not sure. We haven't used the island in years," Annette said, shrugging her shoulders.

Drake placed it aside for later reading, figuring it was a guestbook of some kind for those who visited the cabin in days gone by.

Focusing back upon the weapons, they were immediately familiar with the first bow. The traditional design and impregnated, maple riser told them right away it was a Michigan-made, Predator brand, classic bow. The second one, while being unrecognizable as far as any commercial brand, was of equal quality, other than the green and black spray paint, camouflage job someone had completed on it. That someone, the boys guessed, would have been named Arthur, since that name was the largest writing on the bow, as if the maker wanted everyone to know it was his design and craftsmanship. Multiple other names appeared to be hand-written on the back side of the riser in a silver-ish, almost white color. Doug, Kevin, Darren, Nicholas, Brian, Shaun, Douglas, and Billy were all found to have been scribed on the bow multiple times in various locations. The green bow did not have the same level of craftsmanship as its counterpart, but it was solid in the hand.

The twins and their sister continued their exploration of the safe's contents, also finding an assortment of knives and a few black and white photographs here and there of what seemed to be hunting parties over the years, each of them with multiple animals that did not naturally call the state of Michigan home. Warthogs, impalas, and a few, big jungle cats were enough to let the twins know that their sister was telling the truth about the island's non-human residents.

With the arsenal laid out upon the solid oak, dining room table, the three of them began talking about their plans for sustaining life here on Ascension and how they would stay hidden from the outside world.

"Are you staying with us?" Tomek asked his sister.

"No," she replied. "Not yet, anyway."

"Why not?" Tomek asked, but then kept speaking before letting her answer. "We have everything here we need to live."

"Live happy," Drake added.

"Live together," Tomek said as he completed their plea.

"If I don't go back and deal with the mess that Father Niko just created, they may implicate me and then look for me harder than anyone else. I don't want to bring unwarranted attention to the island," she explained.

"Yea, that makes sense, I guess," said Tomek as he sulked and found himself surprised at the amount of sadness he felt in regards to his older sister leaving them.

"Listen, I have it all figured out. I fly about once every two weeks. I will just make sure I do a couple circles over the island, and I'll drop supplies into the inland lake here. Don't worry. I'll try to get them close to the beach and house, but I will make sure the packages float and are waterproof. The whole damn lake is only three feet deep, so finding them should be easy."

"And what if we need you?" Drake asked.

"There is an extra, portable radio in the plane. I will leave it here, and when I fly over we can talk. I'll get your order for what you need and bring it the following trip out," she explained.

"You really have figured this all out, huh?" Tomek said, showing how impressed he was with his sister's plan.

Annette nodded. "Yea, and if the radio isn't working, just raise the flag."

"So, that is it, huh?" Drake asked. "We just live alone out here from now on?"

"For now, and when or if you ever want to come back, you can. But for now, yes, this is best, I think." Annette sounded more like a mother than a sister at this point.

"How long are you staying?" Tomek asked.

"I filed the flight plan last minute, so they are expecting me back tonight. I will have plenty of questions to answer once I return to Pine Run."

"So, pretty much, you need to leave now?" Drake asked, again finding his sadness in regards to her leaving a peculiar emotion.

"Yup," she replied, turning around and walking out the door.

"So, that is it? You just drop us here on some island and call it good?" Drake challenged her with his question.

"This island has a house, wilder game than you could ever hunt in a lifetime, fishing galore, and most importantly, no people. This is not a prison. It is a blessing, and you would be wise to see it as such. You saved me, and now I have returned the favor. We are square, regardless of what happened underground."

It was the first time the three of them had openly discussed the attempted drowning of the twins by their older sister back in the last home they shared with Uncle.

"I just got one more question for you, Sheriff Henderson," Drake said, using her job title sarcastically.

"Yea, and what is that?"

"Two-ply," Drake said, smiling.

"What?" Henderson said, shrugging her shoulders but full well knowing exactly what she had just heard.

"Two-ply. You know, toilet paper. There is none here, and quite honestly, I have grown quite fond of the stuff," Drake said as he cracked a smile.

"Good thinking." Tomek joined in on the request.

"Of all the things in the world you could request, it's freaking toilet paper that you think you are going to miss the most?" Henderson's face was having trouble hiding a smile of her own.

The boys just looked at each other, shrugged their shoulders, and nodded in agreement.

"Well, I was going to ask for that and a Playboy, but I didn't want to seem too needy," Tomek said, causing both the twins to bust out into full-blown laughter.

"Oh, dear God, you will get your damn toilet paper, but that is it," Henderson said, shaking her head and remembering that, for all that her little brothers were, they were still just teenage boys.

Henderson stood there, looking at them laughing, and felt a twinge of sorrow. In the last forty-eight hours, these boys had killed multiple people, had their home burnt down, and lost everything except each other, again.

The fact that they were happy and laughing only confirmed her decision in regards to placing them on Ascension Island, away from society. In this moment, she knew her actions were not only saving the twins from Pine Run but also Pine Run from the twins.

The List

Ascension Souls.

Friend and Foe. Hunter and Prey.

Chad Bowden

Elliot Hubbard

Terry Akers

Tim Moon

Tom H. - The Ghost

Zane Rhule

Joe Burgess

Bob Young

Jonathan Scharff II

David Berry

Aaron Larson

Ken Scollick

Trevor Johnson

6 ADVENTURE

Watching the small plane taxi out to the far end of the lake, the boys stood on the end of the beach and admired the power in the small engine as it revved up and began its takeoff. Quickly gaining altitude, the plane was off the still, flat, glass-like water and above their heads before they had time to even wave a solemn goodbye. Henderson circled the aircraft around the circular rock walls multiple times, gaining altitude with each pass, until she climbed up and out of the depression. Watching her aerial exit was proof enough to the twins that shooting the gap was a necessary danger when it came to trying to land on the lake.

"Okay, then. Now what?" Tomek asked, looking at his brother.

"We hunt," Drake answered and was delighted with the smile that his words brought across his twin's face.

"You sure?" Tomek asked. "I mean, shouldn't we tour the island and get the lay of the land?"

"We can tour quietly, with bows in our hands, don't you think?" Drake asked, although he was not really looking for an answer.

"Sounds good to me," Tomek replied as they both turned back and began walking up the beach towards the cabin.

Once back inside, the boys were delighted to find the fully stocked cabin contained everything they would need to survive in the wild and even more. Snagging a couple backpacks from where they hung near the door, each twin loaded his own with a various amount of gear they scrounged up from the cabin's interior. Flashlights, food, water bottles, a hatchet, and of course, weapons rounded out their supply list for what they figured would be a good afternoon spent out in the nature of their new home.

Stepping out the front door of the cabin and walking behind the building, the same, sandy trail they had taken up from the beach was evident.

Following that trail for less than a quarter-mile, they quickly found themselves in a dense, pine forest, not unlike the ones near Pine Run. Moving quietly, with their steps covered in the evergreens' discarded needles of seasons gone by, they stayed on the trail, which led them along the outside edge of the pines.

The opposite side of the trail contained what looked to be apple and cherry trees as far as they could see. Beyond the orchard, a large, rock wall jutted up from the ground. From their position on the trail, the moss-covered rocks appeared to be more than fifty feet tall. The presence of both pines and an orchard made both Tomek and Drake feel right at home, but while they were enjoying their stroll amongst the familiar landscapes, there was one thing noticeably missing: animals. There were no signs or tracks of deer, rabbits, or squirrels, and nothing resembling anything weird like they had seen in the pictures back at camp. Aside from a few, normal-looking birds and seagulls, this part of the island seemed dead and void of life.

As they continued moving their way down the trail, both of them fought the urge to hunt in the orchard. Although, the lack of evidence that any wild game actually existed in the area, combined with the elk bugle had come from on top of the plateau, made their decision easier. Knowing that deer would be feasting on the fallen fruit, their desire to follow the trail was based upon the unknown, and when it really boiled down to it, with backpacks and a cabin full of provisions, this trip was more about the adventure than the hunt.

Clearing the pines and orchard, it was clear to see that the rock wall they had seen earlier was more than just a single ledge. The massive structure was the back wall of the same pit that housed their lake and new home and was the very reason why shooting the gap was necessary. Continuing along the trail, they skirted along the massive wall until the trail ended at a large, wooden, plank door that felt clearly out of place. The heavy door, with its wrought-iron castings, appeared to be reinforced and built directly into the rock wall. The back side contained what appeared to be a simple, sliding, iron lock that secured the door when the end of the pole was inserted into a hole drilled into the rock wall.

As if the heavy, wooden, medieval looking door itself was not menacing enough, the hand-carved sign with worn edges and faded, yellow lettering added both mystery as well as a sense of omniscient fear to the door. Reading it aloud, they both pondered on what exactly it meant.

Welcome to the Ascension.

Climb to Heaven and enter the wild.

Those who return alive

Will be amongst the victors.

Those who do not, go onto the list.

"What in the hell does that mean?" Tomek asked, looking at his brother for an answer.

"I have been on this island for as long as you have, so how in the hell am I supposed to know? It seems like we are in some kind of bowl or pit. No way to really know, though. Let's open the door, I guess."

"Great minds think alike," Tomek said, knowing he did not need Drake's permission to open the door but happy nonetheless that they were on the same page.

For the size of the metal locking bar, they both expected it to be heavier, but it slid across the front of the door with a little bit of effort, and the door swung open towards them. Stepping out of the way as the massive door swung by, they both peeked their heads around as it passed by, and while neither one knew what to expect, they both were still surprised at what lay before them.

Steps, lots and lots of steps. The stairway looked as if it had been carved right out of the rock. There were no wood steps or handrail. It was clear that this stairwell and its moss-covered steps had been made so many years ago that any piece of wood would have long since rotted away. The stairwell seemed to go on forever, and at the bottom, looking up, one might actually think that reaching heaven via these steps might be somewhat possible.

"Well, I think we know what the sign meant by 'The Ascension,' " Tomek said as he began walking up the steps.

"Yup," Drake agreed.

Drake pulled the door closed behind them and shut it, noticing a sign on the back of the door as well that matched the one on the opposite side in color and condition. He yelled at his brother to turn around.

"Tomek, look at this."

Welcome back from your attack.
For those who did not fall,
The hunt has changed you all.

"I am starting to think our family may be a little fucked in the head," Tomek said, half laughing and half serious.

"Well, that would certainly explain you," Drake replied, grinning with a smile that made the corners of his mouth reach ear to ear.

"Hilarious," Tomek said, rolling his eyes as he turned to continue his ascent up the stairs.

Climbing the rest of the way in silence, both of the boys marveled at the precision of the stairwell's carving. Not only was the engineering of the steps admirable, so were the walls. A tunnel would have made sense, but there was certainly no ceiling above their heads. They were climbing in what seemed to be a manmade crevice that someone must have blasted out of the rocky, mountain-like wall. For most, this amount of work would have been extremely labor intensive and hard to do. However, now knowing that their family was involved in both the mining and lumber industries, the stairwell was certainly a dream that was made into a reality for someone who could afford to do so.

Reaching the top of the massive stairwell, the twins again found the same, sandy, soiled trail. Only this time, they were presented with two options due to the trailhead quickly forking. Before making their decision, they began to take their surroundings into consideration.

The top of the stairs placed them onto what seemed like level ground. Looking in each direction, they could see no more rock walls, and standing there, looking back over the cliff, the top of the cabin and lake were clearly visible. It was as if the entire island was manmade and sectioned out accordingly.

The east trail headed into a thick forest of hardwood trees, while the west trail bent and disappeared into a large, savannah-like meadow. Separating the two sections of wilderness was a cattail swamp that looked almost as impenetrable as the rock walls itself. The whole top of their new island home was nothing more than a shelf.

"Left or right?" Tomek asked Drake.

"West," Drake replied, turning and pointing out towards the savannah.

"You sure?" Tomek questioned his twin as he wanted clarification.

"Yes, for two reasons," Drake replied.

"Okay, then, I'll bite. What are the two reasons?" Tomek said, giving in to his brother's little game.

"One, if the sun starts going down and it gets dark, we will have the most natural light on the west side of the island."

"And two?" Tomek asked.

"Well, two is quite simple, really," Drake said while pointing down at the ground about fifteen yards ahead of them on the trail.

Walking up to the spot of Drake's focus, both the boys knew what they were looking at.

The elk tracks were a welcome sight and brought a smile to both of their faces. Suddenly, the tracks lent a feeling of familiarity to their strange, new, island home.

"Time to hunt," Tomek said.

Drake looked back at him as he pulled an arrow from the quiver mounted on the side of his bow and agreed with Tomek.

"Yes, sir. Time to hunt."

"Hey, Drake," Tomek said as he too nocked an arrow.

"Yea?" Drake replied, looking back at him.

"Don't call me 'sir.' It is kind of weird," Tomek requested, smiling.

Drake looked back at him with a matching, broken smile of his own and said, "Yes, ma'am."

7 TAIL

Following the elk tracks, Tomek took the lead. Drake did not mind giving up the lead position as he could see in the change of his twin's demeanor that this was what Tomek was born to do. Drake noticed that Tomek moved quietly along the packed sand trail that resembled a typical, northern Michigan, two-track road that would have cut through just about any piece of State land. Each step was made with a full, heal-to-toe, rocking motion that eliminated any sound at all.

Tomek had snagged a cattail head from the wet, swampy area near the trail split and began plucking the hair-like fibers from its brown head. Rubbing his fingers together, he sent them airborne and watched as Mother Nature's breath pushed them away from him and quickly back towards Drake. Having used this method many times before, Tomek knew that the wind was in their favor. He continued trailing the elk with his mind at ease in regards to their scent trail possibly giving away their approach.

Step by step, the boys followed the fresh tracks, not only in an attempt to locate the prey, but also in a continuing attempt to enjoy sightseeing on their new, island home. Pulling the map out from his bag, Drake studied it carefully and was unsure of the overall scale of the island, but was relatively confident that they would be deep into the section labeled as "meadow" soon and still hours from crossing into a top area called "the deep woods." This section being at the complete opposite end of their new home meant that they soon would need to make a decision in regards to heading back to the cabin or staying the night in the wild.

Drake's mind wandered back to the stairwell in the rock wall and the heavy wooden door's message.

"Those who do not, go on the list."

Thinking about that line alone, he also recalled that there was a list of names in the safe's journal that he had set aside, thinking it was a simple guest log.

Perhaps it meant more than just who was on the island, Drake again thought to himself as he watched his brother continue the hunt from behind. Letting his mind run free, he thought, *Maybe, just maybe, that list is those who came to the island before and never left?*

For as removed from this particular hunt as his mind was, the unmistakable sound of a twig breaking up the trail and just around the bend from them was enough to snap him back into the present moment.

Tomek had heard it as well and instantly froze in place. Lowering his shoulders to the ground and sneaking forward with a nocked arrow, he continued in pure stalk mode. Step by step, they hugged the inside corner of the bend in the trail, giving them the advantage of seeing what may lay around the curve before being seen themselves. Both of them utilized the waist-tall, trailside grasses as cover, which meant whatever was around the bend could not see them as they approached within bow range.

Peeking through the swaying grass, their target was identified as they closed the gap. A lone, whitetail doe stood before them at eighteen yards. While Tomek had been hoping to find the elk he was tracking, passing up the chance at some more familiar meat was not something he was going to do. Tomek did not share the fondness for MREs that his brother held. Unaware of their presence, the doe stood there, eating on the trailside greens that had sprouted earlier that spring.

Tomek had enjoyed the stalk and was unsure on his true intentions going forward. At this point in time, they did not really need the meat, and letting her go meant she would be around another day for a future harvest.

After all, when it came down to it, she was stuck on that island the same as them. The towering cliffs and rough waters made sure of that.

Adding to his kill-or-not-kill dilemma was the fact that Annette had mentioned weird wild game to them multiple times. This led to a slight disappointment when the first thing they saw was a normal, Michigan doe. He had hoped that the first animal to have his arrow slice through its lungs would be an impala, kudu, or even possibly a mule deer.

"It is a doe, just a doe," Tomek whispered back to his brother who could clearly see for himself what their quarry at this moment had turned out to be.

"Kill her," Drake said.

"Why? We don't need—" Tomek began to say until Drake interrupted him with a stern look on his face.

"This is our island now, this is our doe now, and we must take our rightful place. You must take her life."

His brother's sudden thirst for blood was confusing and Tomek figured he might as well shoot her to keep Drake happy, being that to him it did not really matter either way. However, their discussion had made killing the doe harder, thanks to her sensing she was no longer alone.

With the wind still in their face, they knew she could not use her greatest survival tool, her nose, to smell them. They also knew that up to this point she could not see them. It really came down to Tomek watching and waiting for her to turn completely broadside, presenting him with a clean, ethical, and easy kill-shot placement into her lungs.

Forcing himself not to blink, in fear that she might see his eyelids close, Tomek watched and waited. What seemed like minutes—if not hours, really—filled the space of just forty-five seconds. The deer turned broadside, revealing her ribcage-protected boiler room, and Tomek raised and canted the bow to his right.

He was unable to draw, thanks to her keen eyesight picking him off as he raised the bow. Tomek remained there on one knee, frozen like a statue in the Pine Run public park. Still, though, she did not blow an emergency call or even bound off, for that matter. She just stared into the bush where he remained crouched, ready to draw. Bobbing her head up and down, the doe attempted to peer into the deep vastness of the bush in an attempt to see exactly what had previously moved. She knew something had caught her eye, just not what that something was.

Drake remained just as frozen as his twin, stuck there watching as the doe stamped her right front leg into the ground with enough force to propel sand from the trail up into the air. Tomek knew that with every warning stomp she made his chances of shooting her drastically went down.

The doe's tongue swung out of her mouth, finding its way up and into her nostrils, lubricating them in an attempt to improve her already impressive sense of smell. Raising her head up in the air to catch the ever present thermals, they both knew that one whiff of human scent, and she would be long gone, with her white flag waving as she bounced off.

Yet just as before, they had the wind in their favor, and with this, the doe relaxed a bit as she appeared to be returning to her previous meal of trailside clover and brassicas. Lowering her head to resume her meal, Tomek felt the string tension on his fingers, but before he could even begin to draw, she whipped her head back up and looked into his bush yet again. She had tricked him.

Clever girl, Drake thought, watching the battle of survival-based wits unfold.

Tomek could not hear his brother's thoughts, but he knew exactly what they were. Uncle had told them about this behavior many times, saying only the oldest and wisest of the does will pull off this type of fake, relaxed, head-swing move. There was only on way to counteract it, and Tomek remembered Uncle's exact words. Tomek heard Uncle's voice again in his head for the first time in a while.

"Watch her tail, not her head."

Uncle would explain what he meant by saying, *"She will lower her head in that fake motion as many as ten times. But only when she flicks her tail and then lowers her head will it stay down. Watch the tail, not the head. When it flicks, that is your chance."*

Taking heed to Uncle's lesson, both twins remained stationary and watched as the deer bobbed and weaved her head like a city-corner prizefighter who cared more about trash talking than throwing blows. But then it happened. Just like Uncle said it would, her tail flicked, and as she dropped her head, Tomek drew back the Predator recurve bow. Anchoring his draw hand deep into the natural pocket created by his well-defined cheekbone, Tomek held the string steady.

Hearing Uncle's voice again, he tried to focus on a single hair in her hide.

"Four inches up the leg, two inches back, my son. Aim small, miss small."

Tomek had reached full draw and found his anchor point. He aimed small and released the string feeling the twine burn as it drug across his loose finger tips. Tomek watched the bright fletching spin as the arrow connected into the broadside body of the doe.

He turned around to look at his brother, expecting a celebratory hug or high five, but with a quick glance he knew something was wrong. Drake's eyes were bigger than he had ever seen, and it was almost as if he could see movement in the reflection of his twin's pupil.

Spinning back around, the fear that his brother's face had exposed instantly hit him as well. Forty yards away, charging in a full-out, bolting sprint was the largest, cat-like creature either of them had ever seen. With each paw that slammed into the ground, propelling its massive body towards them, the male, African lion's thick, multiple shaded mane with its matching tail puff bounced as if it was in slow motion. It was not until the king of beasts was a mere ten yards away that they both turned to run.

With each brother splitting into an opposite direction, there was no thinking, only reacting. Lions don't wait for tail flicks; lions just attack. With no time to plan or even fight, the twins just fled. Drake headed deep into the thick, waist-tall, meadow grassland area, turning south towards the Ascension steps. Tomek dropped the bow and turned east in a dead sprint for the only landmark he saw that might provide some form of protection. A tall oak tree, on the edge of the cliff, stood resolute and alone. There was not a single branch within reach and no way to climb it; but Tomek had no other options, and his survival instinct just said, "*RUN!*"

Luckily for both of the twins, the smell of the blood-stained ground where Tomek's arrow had sliced its way through the chest, severing the heart and lungs of the doe, combined with their splitting of ways confused the lion. Stopping his charge for a few seconds to test the wind, just like the doe, he too found it useless in locating the boys and with Drake hidden in the grass and the deer dead at the end of its blood trail, the lion turned his attention to the only prey he had a visual on: Tomek.

Tomek had opened an impressively large gap of distance on the cat as he headed for the oak tree. Nearing the behemoth of a tree, he glanced back, hoping to not see a lion at all, but if there was one there, he hoped it would still be far off. Shockingly, he did see the lion, and even more shockingly, he knew that in a just a few pounces, the brute would have closed the distance, making him nothing more than the pride's next meal.

Tomek lowered his head as every single ounce of adrenalin dumped into his bloodstream, and he felt his legs push against the ground through the grips on the bottom of his boots as they tore against the dirt in his feeble attempt to outrun a lion. Tomek knew he was no deer, no gazelle, nor even impala. Tomek knew he was dead. The tree was now just ahead of him, just like the cliff. At this point, he was unsure what the better option was. He knew he couldn't out-climb a cat, let alone outrun it, and jumping off the cliff meant certain death, thanks to the jagged rocks and lake seven stories below.

One day—one day on this rock and I am dead already. This really is a fucking prison. She never meant for it to be a home, Tomek thought to himself.

Reaching the base of the tree, he jumped over one of the exposed roots that were anchoring the tree into the top shelf of the island, keeping the oak from falling over the cliff. The trunk extended straight up, and Tomek knew his only hope was to try and shim up it somehow.

He glanced one last time behind him, in preparation for his climb, only to find the lion completely airborne with not a single paw on the ground. Every hair of the lion's mane brushed back with the acceleration of his final, death pounce, and the cat flew forward towards Tomek with each of his razor-like claws exposed.

Tomek bent down, loading every ounce of energy he could muster into his hamstrings, quadriceps, and calves. Reeling in the stored tension, Tomek sprang forward at the base of the tree. Feeling his foot make contact with the rough bark, he arched his back and pushed off of the tree again as if he had been a gymnast his entire life. Tomek was suddenly eight feet in the air, arching backwards. His legs straightened out as his reverse momentum aided the back flip he had just completed over the top of the lion. Passing up and over the lion, his face brushed against the top of the cat's ears, and the strong, unfamiliar odor nearly caused what little he had in his stomach to lurch out. The musty, ammonia-rich musk of the lion, combined with the iron metallic smell of fresh blood, would now be forever ingrained in his mind. He did not know where the blood smell came from, only that it was not his blood, and at the moment, he was happy for that.

The cat turned in midair as the surprise of his quarry's agility caused him to swipe upwards, missing Tomek completely. Although most cats land on their feet, this one did not. Slamming down into the loose gravel near the edge of the cliff, the cat slid towards the ledge. His weight played against him this time as he slid off the edge but did not fall, thanks to the extension of his right front paw, whose claws had buried themselves deep into a stray root from the oak tree.

Hanging off the edge, the king let loose an angry roar, and Tomek wasted no time in removing the hatchet he had picked up in the cabin. Cocking it back, Tomek slammed the blade down deep into the paw, severing it so badly that the blade of the weapon lodged itself deep into the wood of the root. Tomek's counter attack had removed not only the lion from the majority of his paw but the lion from the island completely.

Looking over the edge, Tomek was unsure of what he would see, but it was obvious the rocks had completed the job that Tomek set in motion. The black rocks, adorned in green lichens and moss, were now painted a crimson red. Covered in the cat's blood, Tomek knew that for at least now he was alive. At least now he was safe, but he needed to find Drake.

Looking down, he picked up the hatchet, using all of his body weight against the handle to remove it from the section of root he had split. Lying there next to the split root was Tomek's first true trophy of Ascension Island. Much like the rib of the first hunter he killed on the banks of Uncle's river home and much like the green, Lucky Trail uniform shirt he still had on, this kill provided him with a keepsake.

Tomek bent down and picked up the only piece of the lion that remained on the island. A four-inch-long claw and held it tight.

Standing at the edge of the cliff, facing the interior of the island and looking at all that lay before him, Tomek was overcome with both rage and pride. Thumping one closed fist against his chest in an aggressive, syncopated manner that would have hurt in normal circumstances, he raised the severed lion's claw into the sky and let loose a roar of his own, followed by a primal yell.

"This. Is. My. Island!"

8 NIGHT

For those who did not fall,
The hunt has changed you all.

The boys again read these words on the back of the large, wood door as they reached the bottom of the rock stairwell, and both now realized exactly how true they were. All they had ever learned about the outdoors, about life, about death, and about hunting had been forever changed. The words on the door were never truer than at this moment.

"Well, I certainly did not 'fall.' The lion did," Tomek said in a somewhat boastful manner, pointing at the verse on the door.

"Yea, but that was close," Drake responded in a sobering tone.

"Too close," Tomek agreed. "Think she knew?"

Drake shrugged his shoulders. "Knew what?"

"About there being a damn lion up there," Tomek said, making his question clearer.

"Maybe. I mean, she did say there was weird stuff. But I don't see a hippo in the lake, and she mentioned that, too," Drake rationalized, not wanting to think that perhaps their sister had once again stranded them to die. "Maybe she has never even been to the top of the steps? Maybe she had no idea the steps existed? She said that she hadn't been here since she was a kid, after all."

"Well, you know what I think?" Tomek said, not waiting for Drake to answer his rhetorical question. "I think that bitch dropped us here, knowing that we wouldn't be on the top of the fucking food chain."

47

"A little dramatic, don't you think?" Drake asked, not looking for an answer but making a point.

"Dramatic, my ass," Tomek replied as he opened the door to the cabin and sat down at the large, dining room table.

"Well, when she comes back, I guess we will just have to ask her then, huh?"

"When?" Tomek scoffed. "I think you mean *if.*"

"When, if—whatever," Drake said, hoping he was right about the eventual return of their sister. "All I know right now, after one day here, is that we have enough food to last all winter without having to climb those steps."

"And then what?" Tomek asked.

"We garden and fish. And that's only if she doesn't come back," Drake answered.

"Well, be that as it may, I killed that doe, and tomorrow we are going up there to get our meat."

"Why not just go get her now then?" Drake asked full well knowing that Tomek would not be looking forward to blood trailing in the dark on an island that contained lions. Drake placed a hand on Tomek's shoulder and turned him around as he looked at his brother and saw something in his eyes that told him this was not worth discussing. Drake knew his brother would climb those stairs in the morning with or without him, and Drake knew that meant he would have to as well. Silence fell between the two of them as each one devoured the first MRE of their stay on Ascension Island.

In an attempt to break the silence, as well as change the topic of their last conversation, Drake cleared his throat and motioned out the window. "What kind of fish do you think are in this lake?"

"I don't know. It's an inland lake, so maybe the normal pan fish and bass type stuff," Tomek guessed.

"Yea, but if there is a lion and stuff at the top of the stairs, who knows what is swimming out there," Drake said.

"The lion or lions can survive the winter, I imagine. I don't see tropical fish, or whatever you're thinking about, doing the same." Tomek again seemed to be skeptical about the aquatic residents of the lake. "That being said, since you asked, there might be lake trout or salmon in there. I don't know, but we should check it out tomorrow."

However, it was not his remarks on the absence of weird fish that caught Drake's attention. It was a single word that Tomek had said that made Drake both excited and scared at the same time.

"Lions?" Drake said as he raised his voice at the end of the word, asking his brother if he thought there were more without having to bring himself to say it.

"I don't know," Tomek replied. "But there is one less now, and if there are not any more, then that means hopefully my doe will last through the night without getting eaten."

Clearing the rest of their meal packets and placing them in a trash bin, they stepped back outside and watched as the sun began to sink behind the rock wall's jagged, top ledge. Walking the dirty sand path down to the beach, the twins stood near a fire pit that had been excavated in the sand and outlined with large, perfectly spherical, white rocks. Looking at the fire pit, the brothers began collecting tinder from the grassy areas around the beach. Tomek then grabbed a heaping armload of the split firewood that had been neatly stacked in rows against the east side of the cabin.

Without having to mention it, they both realized that, for all they had been through in just one day, they both were happy to be alive and on the island. For what Pine Run and Old Man Hawkins had provided them in a sense of comfort and assimilation, it robbed from them their sense of freedom, spirit, and survival.

Quickly, the fire was lit, and as the shadows upon the lake grew longer with the fading sunlight, much of the world fell silent. Even the gentle lapping of the water as it came ashore had settled down and given way to a chorus of frogs and crickets. It was not the same as the peaceful flowing of their old river home, but it held many of the same qualities.

The twins sat there in a set of folding, aluminum lawn chairs, whose checkered seat weavings had seen better days thanks to both dry rot and the chewing of mice. They found the chairs stuffed under the porch, and with their feet in the sand, they sipped on the bitter coffee that had been made with the grounds that came in each of their MREs. It certainly was not the Mason Jar Coffee Company quality brew that Old Man Hawkins sold in the store that they had become accustomed to, but on Ascension Island this was better than nothing.

Sitting there, rubbing their hands together and holding them up to the flames in an attempt to warm them, Drake looked at his brother in the flickering light, and for a multitude of reasons that made zero sense, all felt right in the world. There was something about the popping snap of the pine sap oozing from within the logs they burnt that added to the ambiance of the night. The flickering light, waves of heat, and the glowing embers of a red-hot coal bed all combined together to create this very tranquil moment.

Looking up at the stars that Mother Nature had laid before them, Drake thought of Uncle. He wondered how Uncle would have handled their situation on this island prison. He knew that Uncle not only would have survived, but that he would have been happy here. Closing his eyes, he cleared his mind and blocked out everything around him. He blocked out the croaking of the bullfrogs and the rhythmic chirping of the crickets. He blocked out the gentle lapping of the shoreline waves and even the slight breeze. Drake became one with himself in this moment and entered a settled stream of consciousness. It was only then that he again heard his beloved

Uncle's voice.

"The happiest people don't have the best of everything. They just make the best of everything they have."

Tomorrow would be a new day, a new adventure. Yet to Drake, one thing was for certain: No matter what happened tomorrow at the top of those stairs, they were back. Back in the woods, back in the water, back in the wild. The twins were finally home.

9 FLOATING

The rising sun over the eastern horizon was a welcome sight to Garran Barr as he sat in his captain's chair aboard the cockpit of his precious *Full Coverage*. With a new day upon them, Barr knew that, after stopping in Traverse City later tonight for fuel and supplies, they would soon be headed directly to their hunting grounds.

"Are we there, yet?" Tony, his son, joked with a yawn as he entered the cabin area.

"Fourteen hours to Traverse City, my boy."

"Oh, that's all?" his son quipped back.

"I am picking up on your sarcasm there, T-man," Garran said.

Tony just laughed with an exaggerated eye-roll and said, "Well, I certainly hope so, 'cause I am laying it on pretty thick."

The two Barrs enjoyed a good laugh as Garran thought there may be no better way to start a day than sunrise with your boy on the boat.

"Where in the hell is breakfast?" Sven shouted from below, interrupting the father-son moment the Barrs were previously enjoying.

"Make something," Garran yelled back at Sven, again flashing a smile to his son.

"What?" Sven replied.

"Make your own damn breakfast. What do you think this is? A Carnival cruise ship?" Garran intensely scorned back.

"Well, no, this ain't no damn cruise ship, for sure. I just thought you knew how to be a good host."

"Okay, Elliot," Greggor said, joining the conversation.

Greggor's comment caused the adults all to laugh as Tony sat there with a courtesy smile. He could not help but to think he had missed out on some sort of an inside joke.

The rest of the group joined Garran in the cockpit and enjoyed the rising of the sun while sipping coffee out of mason jars.

"Hey, Captain, ever heard of a coffee cup?" Ricardo asked Garran in regards to the mason jars in their hands.

"You are drinking the finest brew Michigan has to offer, from The Mason Jar Coffee Company. You drink it from the jar out of respect. Got it?"

The crew got it, and while they didn't fully understand the answer, they didn't really care, because the coffee was truly excellent.

The mood was light as each of them nursed a mixture of sea sickness with the residual hangovers from their libations the night before.

"So, what is the plan Capi-tan?" Archer said, emphasizing the rhyme in his question.

However, before Garran could answer his new deckhand's question, Ricardo barged in and stated, "Well, first, we get rid of the rhyming poet."

The group laughed, all looking at Archer and waiting for his response, which was the perfect comeback.

"You don't like me being a poet? Hey, I didn't know it."

Again, the men busted out laughing at their newfound, poet friend. Barr then answered the original question.

"We have an all-day steam ahead of us. If the wind and waves cooperate, then we should reach the tip of Grand Traverse Bay around ten o'clock tonight. We will stay there, fuel up, feed up, and then tomorrow we will head out to Ascension."

"An all-day steam—oh, God, this coffee needs some more cream," Archer exuberated. But this time, he found his comedic timing to be off as not a single guy in the group so much as cracked a smile.

"Okay, let's throw his ass into the lake," Ricardo demanded, causing all the laughter that had been sucked out of the room to return.

"Nah, we won't toss him just yet, but he did just earn himself cook duty for the day," Garran said. "Tony, go down there, show him where the kitchen stuff is, and help him out, will ya?"

Although cooking breakfast for the guys with Archer was the last thing Tony wanted to do, he knew that, being this was his first trip, he had to earn his keep as well as keep his dad and the guys happy to make sure that he would be invited back again.

Tony and Archer exited the cabin area, and as they did, Sven closed the door behind them, leaving the three Stratton brothers alone with Garran.

Looking over his shoulder, out the porthole sized window, to make sure the coast was clear, Greggor looked back to Barr and asked, "Do you think he knows?"

"Who? Archer or Tony?" Barr replied.

"Well, honestly, either, but more so Archer. His name is the one going on the list, after all," Greggor said.

"No, he has no clue. We have sold it good," said Barr.

"You sure? Because he may be a little bit older than Elliot was, but he is in pretty damn good shape," said Sven.

"What? You afraid of a little challenge?" Ricardo said, raising an eyebrow at his younger brother.

"No, I am not afraid, but—" Sven mumbled, before being interrupted.

"But what? Archer is not Elliot," Greggor said, trying to calm them down.

"Listen, I know Elliot gave us more of a challenge than we expected on the island. He was big and slow, so we all underestimated him. And the bastard had a ton of experience in the outdoors. There was no way for us to know that. Just as we underestimated his size, let's not overestimate Archer based on his," Garran said, taking a deep breath before he continued. "But you have to remember one thing. Where is Elliot's name now?"

"It's on the list," Sven answered, nodding his head.

"Exactly," Garran said. "And is your name on the list?"

"No," Sven said.

"And is *your* name on the list?" Garran said, motioning over to Ricardo.

"Never going to happen, my friend," Ricardo replied.

"And what about you, Greggor? Is your name on the list?" Garran asked the last remaining Stratton.

"Negative, Captain," Greggor replied.

Sven spoke at this point and said, "Okay, okay. You have made your point." While everyone in the cabin was satisfied with the ending of this particular discussion, Sven still had his doubts. "When do we tell Tony?"

"We don't tell Tony," Garran said, speaking of his son.

"How do we not tell him?" Greggor asked.

"*We* don't. *I* do. He is my son, and I know he is ready for the hunt. In fact, I think he might get the kill. That kid may be young, but he is agile, fast, and full of piss and vinegar."

"Think he can outrun a bear?" Greggor asked.

"Fuck the bear. Do you think he can outrun the lion?" Ricardo added to the question list facing Garran in regards to the effectiveness of his son on the hunt.

"Listen, that kid is faster than you, stronger than you, and smarter than all of you combined," said Garran, defending his son against the Stratton brothers, only half joking.

"Yea, that he is, but we all know that hunting on Ascension has just as much to do with your head as it does your body," Sven retaliated as he pressed his index finger into his temple.

"If it was all mental, then why are you so good at it, shit for brains?"

Ricardo said, picking on Sven.

The joke made by Ricardo at Sven's expense lightened the mood and the four of them broke up the small meeting in the cabin, each going their own ways and settling in for the long trip up to Traverse City.

The rest of the day was relatively uneventful. The group lounged around, watching movies on the big screen, and even stopped for a big lake swim after lunch. The trip up Michigan's west coast was full of sparkling, blue and green waters that plunged to mystic and dark, unthinkable fathoms. With little to no wind and wave chop, the *Full Coverage* made good time, and not long after watching the sun vanish in spectacular fashion into the seemingly never-ending west side of the Lake Michigan horizon, the group motored into the bay at Traverse City, finding their rented dock slip and settling in at the marina. A quick glance at the radar made Garran happy that he had made it into the bay when they did.

"Want to head into town for drinks?" Archer asked Garran, upon shoring up the lines on the stern of the vessel.

As much as Garran thought a night on the town with the boys would be enjoyable, he knew better than to chance it as he looked at the weather report.

"Nah, there is one hell of a bad storm system out towards the middle of the lake. We need to get all the tie downs on and make sure they are secure. This looks like it could be a rough night, and we have some work to do. Plus, if it blows over, we can head out in the morning with an early start."

"Aye, aye, Captain," Archer responded in a mocking sailor voice as he continued his boat work. His playful demeanor made Barr smile and shake his head at the goofball.

Garran left the cabin and joined the others, who had gathered in the media room and were already enjoying their first round of drinks. Entering the room, Garran felt the mood change instantly, and he knew something was up. The Stratton brothers sat around the poker table with Tony, and all of them had fallen silent as they looked up at Garran.

"What?" Garran asked, wondering what in the hell was going on.

However, no one had to tell him what was up as he made eye contact with Tony. The look on his son's face told him all he needed to know. While Garran was not sure which of the Stratton brothers had let the truth slip, he knew that one of them had done just that.

Tony Barr now knew the horrific details of what his first hunt on Ascension Island would actually be. Tony was told how the island was home to many species of animals, many of which could—and would—easily kill him. If that was not enough to jar him to his core and make him fear for his life, the target species on this particular hunt was the most dangerous game of all. Tony sat there in silence, looking at his father. Again, the look in his eyes asked all the questions his mouth and mind could not.

Garran walked over to the table, stood across from this son in a dramatic notion, and just nodded, as if he was confirming everything the Stratton brothers had just told his son. He was not happy with the brothers and their big mouths, but he knew at this point none of that mattered. Garran needed to focus on the reaction of his son and not on the anger he felt swell inside towards his shipmates. Garran knew exactly why they had told Tony now. It was a simple test. If the kid cracked overnight with this new information, then he would crack on the island under the pressure of life and death. Either way, there could be no cracks on their team. Cracks had always led to the wrong names ending up on the list.

Embracing Tony against his chest, he pulled the boy close and said, "Son, the lions will hunt you. The bears will hunt you. The dogs will hunt you. The island will hunt you. But you—you will hunt, and you will kill Archer."

10 MEADOW

While the *Full Coverage* motored its way towards Traverse City, the island home of the boys basked in the same, beautiful and perfect, pure Michigan sunrise that had graced the shorelines of the Lower Peninsula. The twins woke with a new sense of vigor and wonder. However, they were not completely on the same page.

Grabbing a bow and quiver, Tomek loaded a few MREs into a brown, leather backpack he had found in the closet and stepped out the door.

"Where in the hell are you going?' Drake asked, knowing the answer.

"Tracking."

Tomek's one-word reply was enough for Drake to get annoyed. "Don't you think we could spend one day—just one damn day—not defending our lives?" Drake asked his brother.

"I have a doe down. It is time to go find her," Tomek replied as if climbing the stairs and heading out into the wilds of Ascension Island was no big deal.

"What about the lions?" Drake reminded him.

"I killed the lion."

"I said *lions*, with an *s*," Drake responded, again knowing his brother knew his concerns but unsure if Tomek's bravado was real or if it was purely based on fear.

In the short time since the Sheriff and his squad had hunted them in the woods, Drake had noticed a change in his brother. Drake was sure he had changed as well, but trying to look at the situation objectively, he preferred his method of coping to Tomek's. When it came to fear or danger, Drake had become smarter and more calculated in dealing with each issue, while his twin had resorted to unadulterated violence. Acting like the alpha predator in every situation was Tomek's new modus operandi. Of course, Drake did have to give his brother some credit. They were still alive, and anyone who had challenged them was not. Still, they had plenty to survive in the camp, and Drake saw no reason for now to go up top. With fertile soil behind the cabin and a lake full of fish, there was no need to hunt today or for weeks. Tomek was not going on a substance hunt; he was looking for trophies.

"I have killed one lion—one, big, fucking lion—and if there is more than one, I won't be surprised. I will be ready for them," Tomek said as he threw the leather pack up over his shoulder.

"You really think it is going to be that easy, huh?" Drake asked.

Tomek just gave his twin a little, smartass grin and replied, "For me, yes. For you, not so much."

"Well, what is your plan?"

"I don't make plans. That's your job," Tomek replied.

"Well, my plan is to figure out what kind of fishing action there is here in this little lake. Then, I am going to check out that back, grassy area with the waist-high fence. That had to be some kind of a garden or orchard years ago, and if there is a fence, then there must be rabbits to hunt."

Drake was proud of his answer and hoped it was detailed enough to convince his brother to remain lakeside with him at the bottom of the steps.

"Wrong plan. Better start working out what we are going to do once we find my doe," Tomek scoffed.

"We?"

"Yes, *we*. I am going up there in five minutes, and we both damn well know you're not going to let me go alone. And, well, since I don't see a whole lot of other people around for you to send with me—guess what—you are climbing those steps."

"I hate it when you are right," Drake said, passing Tomek at a faster pace and bumping his shoulder into his brother's as he entered the cabin to gear up.

Jumping into battle situations seemed almost a regular occurrence to both of them at this point, and it was less than ten minutes later that Drake had scrounged up enough supplies and a bow of his own. The attached quiver housed a full array of razor-sharp, metal-headed arrow shafts with larger, shield cut fletching than he was used to. The inscription on the inside of the lower limb near the riser of his new weapon read "JV Outback." While it was not the recurve he was used to, he felt this bow would be a fine replacement.

"Okay, let's go," Drake said, motioning to Tomek.

"Nah, I changed my mind. Let's just go swimming," Tomek replied in an attempt to annoy his twin.

"Har, har," Drake said as he followed Tomek out the front door. They quickly made their way through the pines and into the garden area that buffered up against the rock wall and the steps.

This time, climbing up the steps into Ascension Island seemed easier. After all, they had a better grasp on what to expect; although honestly, last time, neither of them had expected a lion.

Reaching the top of the steps, they again faced a dilemma.

"Do you really want to track that doe, or should we go explore some more?" Drake asked.

"Let's head up this way on this trail to the left. We know where I shot her and where I killed the lion," Tomek suggested.

"So, we are going to ignore this trail to the right?"

"We have the map you pulled out of that book, right?" Tomek asked.

"Yeah."

"Well, it looks like to me that the place is basically a circle, and all the paths lead back to the steps," Tomek said.

"Dude, you know damn well this is the exact same thing I told you last night before bed," Drake said, rolling his eyes.

"Yup. It made sense then, so why not now?" Tomek asked, not really wanting an answer but more so just making a point.

Drake did not answer him as they continued walking slowly up the west trail through the same, slightly undulating, open meadow area where they had shot the deer on the previous day. While they had passed the shot site about an hour earlier, they were now both enjoying their exploration mission.

Reaching the top of a hill and cresting the apex near the very northern tip of the island, Drake grabbed his brother's shoulder from behind, pulling him down low to the ground in a crouching position, and whispered, "I'm guessing we are not going to find your doe."

"Oh, really, tracker boy? What makes you think that?" Tomek asked.

Drake didn't answer. He just nodded forward into the open meadow. Down to their right, towards the interior of the island, Tomek spotted what Drake was referencing, and he agreed about the outcome of his kill.

In the very dead center of the meadow, among the short grasses and the most beautiful mix of purple, white, and yellow wildflowers they had ever seen, was the biggest bear either of them had ever laid eyes upon. The bruin feasted on what looked to be the doe that Tomek had killed the day before. The very doe the bear ripped apart effortlessly before them may have been the same one that ultimately led to the death of what was perhaps this brown bear's biggest rival on the island in the lion. Upon reaching his stomach's full point, the beast dropped down next to the remaining carcass and rolled to his back. Extending his legs outward, he exposed the weapon-like claws that adorned each paw. With one, large exhale, the twins watched as the fat and happy bear dozed off for a midday siesta right there in the middle of the meadow without a care in the world.

"Can you believe he is just crashing for a nap right there?" Drake asked.

"That is an animal with no predators. His brown ass thinks he is king of this island," Tomek replied.

"Well, if—and it is a big 'if'—but if there was only one lion, then yea, he pretty much is the king I'd say," claimed Drake, knowing that the reply would annoy Tomek, who was trying to make the point that they were the new kings.

"I bet he is happy that Cecil took a leap of faith then," Tomek joked.

Drake looked at his brother in confusion and whispered back inquisitively, "Cecil?"

"Yea, Cecil. The lion I sent over the cliff," Tomek replied in a matter-of-fact manner.

"You named the fucking lion?" Drake asked while rolling his eyes with a sigh.

"Sure did."

Drake left the line of questioning alone there as he was not surprised at his brother's naming of the lion, but he also didn't really care. He just knew that today appeared to be a good day to be a bear on Ascension Island.

"Grizzly?" Tomek asked his brother.

"That, or a Kodiak. I mean, I am not sure, but I know that ain't no Michigan black bear."

Drake kept his hand firmly still on the back of Tomek's shoulder. Drake could feel Tomek slightly and involuntarily tremble a little bit with each breath. He slightly tugged on his brother's shirt and motioned to him that they retreat back down the hill.

"But he has my kill," Tomek said in feeble attempt to show he wasn't afraid of the bear.

"It is his now, and we have the wind. Let's circle around. We know he is here, and he has no idea we exist. Another day, bro. We will hunt him another day," Drake whispered while walking back down the hill, down the trail leading back towards the wall.

"Yea," Tomek said. "Another day."

Working their way back through the meadow, the boys enjoyed the natural breeze that this secluded landmass in the middle of the Great Lakes provided. Their trip down the winding, meadow path provided breathtaking, cliff-side, panoramic views, and they both felt not only lucky to be alive but lucky to be alive on Ascension. Upon reaching the wall, they quickly realized that it was past lunch time, and their trip up to the north side of their new home had taken more time than they had expected. Lunch was spent talking about bears, lions, and, yes, even Uncle. The boys talked about how much he would have enjoyed the island and how this was the first place they had ever been that sounded anything like the Hawaiian Islands that Uncle spoke fondly of.

With the sun at its highest point in the sky and their day half over, it was decision time.

"Want to head back down, catch some fish or swim or something?" Drake suggested.

This time, Tomek was the one rolling his eyes. "Negative."

"Yea, I figured that. You want to go hunt down the sleeping bear, don't ya?" Drake asked, thinking he had his twin pegged.

To his surprise, Tomek just shook his head.

"Negative."

"Well, okay then. We got half a day and some fancy new arrows. What's the plan?" Drake asked, not really caring about what they did to fill the rest of their sunlight.

"This is our home, and we have only seen half of it. Who knows what else is out here. Let's go for a hike," Tomek replied, pointing past the entrance to the steps leading down from the wall.

"Yea, maybe the east side of this prison island has polar bears," Drake said with a grin.

"Don't be ridiculous," Tomek replied. "Polar bears live in Antarctica."

"They sure do, and lions live in Africa."

Tomek shrugged his shoulders and agreed, "Good point."

11 LAUGHS

Cleaning up from their lunch, the twins headed south along the trail, skirting the wall. While they both were not surprised in regards to the cliff-side beauty of the island's east side, they were slightly taken aback by the difference in vegetation. After passing alongside a few miles of a deep hardwoods patch, the two-track, manmade trail turned back north into the woods, and the twins found themselves surrounded in what felt like home.

The relatively flat woods consisted mostly of oak, pine, and maples, and as they explored miles deep into what they felt was the heart of the island, the height and overall vastness of the canopy above them drowned out the sunlight. Tomek and Drake knew it was well into the middle of a bright, sunny day, but inside the island's forest it was already an eerie twilight. Moving along the woodlot's open floor line were piles and piles of perfectly round rock formations that were almost fully covered in green moss. This drew the curiosity of the twins. Being too perfect in shape to be anything other than manmade, the twins cleared out the back side of each pile and made sure nothing was behind them, hiding in wait for them. Doing so with drawn bows, they tactically circled each formation, thinking they would make for the perfect ambush spot for a predator.

Well aware of the island's dangers they had encountered so far, each step was taken with caution. While they were armed with their bows, arrows nocked, they knew that on Ascension they were not the top of the food chain. The wide, sandy trail they had enjoyed on the island's opposite side all but vanished inside their current location. Years of wet and decomposing leaf-cover, combined with a solid bed of pine needles, laid cover to the only thing on the island that was consistent: the trail.

"I think we are way off the path," Tomek said as the reached the inside edge of the woodlot and stood there overlooking a marshy swamp bog that was reminiscent of every nasty, muck tar pit they had ever read about in Hawkins' old collection of encyclopedias.

"You're just now figuring that out?" Drake replied. "Let's just start heading back towards the lake on this side of the island. We can follow the coastline back to the cabin or keep working our way back to the top."

"What time is it, you think?" Tomek asked.

"Don't worry about it. We have plenty of time to reach the top and get back if we move now," Drake said as he started marching back into the damp darkness of the tree cover.

"Well then," Tomek quipped as he followed his brother.

It was not long before they were again at the edge of the hardwood section and now staring over an undulating valley of ferns that stretched all the way to the coastline's drop off.

"Didn't expect to see this," Tomek said.

"Yea, me either. This freaking place has a little bit of everything," Drake replied. "Not as nice out anymore. Feel that wind?"

Tomek agreed. "I was just going to say the same thing. Must be a storm coming tonight."

"Yea, but we're in the middle of a huge-ass lake. Who knows how quick it could roll in? I mean, they hit Oscoda quick once the cell is up, and that's the mainland. Out here, well, out here we have no idea," Drake said.

"Yup. Best we head back to the cabin and wait it out."

Tomek's passive suggestion surprised his brother. While Drake agreed with his twin, his own desire to push forward and see the rest of the island was very strong.

The twins began bushwhacking their way through the knee-high ferns, and upon cresting the top of a small rise, they both smiled as they looked down and saw the road just thirty five yards below them in the bottom of another coolie. Making quick work of the remaining ferns between them and the road, Drake and Tomek stopped to rest and drink from their canteens.

"Well do you really want to head back or keep going?" Drake asked.

"It's up to you, but if we stay out, you know damn well we're going to be getting wet," Tomek replied.

"What? You afraid of getting a little wet?" asked Drake.

"Not at all. Just do not want you to melt, sugar plum," Tomek replied, mocking his brother.

And with that, the boys were again walking the trail to the north as a light, drizzling rain began to spatter here and there. The valley of the ferns was reminiscent of the many valleys they originally called home in the happy days spent with Uncle. Although it was not that long ago in actual time, it seemed to them both that those days—happy days—were a lifetime ago.

Working their way up a hillside and out of the valley, the twins had let their guard down and progressed through the area with less caution. Being out in the open, they were well aware that any animal predator would be able to spot them, but they also knew they would be able to see the attack coming and prepare for it. They took their safety cue from the multitude of deer that were quietly and peacefully feeding in the area. One such buck had gotten so close to them they wondered if it was somewhat tame.

"Was that a muley?" Tomek asked.

"You mean a mule deer?" Drake replied.

"You know what the hell I mean, yeah."

"Had to be, because its antlers went up and out, not up and forward. Plus, look at the way it is hopping. Whitetails never run like that," Drake said as he confirmed his brother's suspicions.

Watching the deer that was foreign to Michigan, the boys couldn't help but again wonder about Uncle. Drake was the first to mention him aloud.

"You know, he would have really loved it here."

Not needing to mention exactly who his brother was talking about, Tomek simple nodded and said, "Yep."

Reaching the end of the fern valley, the boys were able to glance over the cliffs again and look out to the lake.

"Well, that does not look good," Drake said of the dark, wall cloud forming and seemingly hurtling its way towards them.

"How long till it hits us?" Tomek asked.

"No idea for sure, but I would guess about an hour and a half or so," Drake replied. "Let's head back. Even the deer have left the valley."

"Sounds good," Tomek agreed, knowing that time spent sitting out a storm of this magnitude would be much nicer in the safety and comfort of the cabin, which also had the advantage of being protected from the raging winds that were sure to accompany the rain and lightning.

With the wind picking up, there was a noticeable difference in the temperature drop, and it was as if all the hair on the back of their necks and arms stood up at once. Both trusting their instincts, the boys turned to head back down into the valley towards shelter and within three steps knew that taking the trail south all the way would no longer be an option.

Just over one hundred yards away, seven dog-like creatures just barely taller than the surrounding ferns emerged from the green, fern tops. Slinking into the roadway with their noses to the ground, it was clear they were on the trail of the boys' scent.

Dropping to a crouch while looking down at what was in front of them, Tomek turned to Drake and said, "That explains the lack of deer remaining in the field."

"Too big to be coyotes," Drake remarked.

"Yea. Too organized, as well. And they ain't hairy enough to be wolves," Tomek remarked.

Before either twin could glance another peek, they clearly heard the dog-like pack of hunters now only forty yards away. Upon hearing the distinct, loud, and high pitched yip-like cackle of the approaching pack, they looked at each other and at the exact same time said, "Hyenas."

Tomek looked at Drake and silently motioned out the drawing of a bow. Drake nodded and motioned with his fingers: One. Two. Three.

Standing up and drawing their bows, both Tomek and Drake were ready to take on the hyena cackle, but to their dismay and albeit relief, the pack had vanished into the ferns just as quick as they had magically appeared.

Scanning the field from left to right, not a single devil dog could be seen. However, the relentless cackles and yelps helped the twins locate their approximate locations. Walking away from the majority of the yelps, backwards to the top of the last hill they had yet to crest, it was obvious the pack was on them. Circling the twins, the hyenas' obnoxiously sinister laughter was enough to make any man fall apart. Every few seconds, the twins caught movement underneath the surrounding ferns as the African dogs skimmed the top edge. The ferns swaying unpredictably, thanks to the steady winds of the storm front quickly making its way inland from the islands coast, combined with the fact that the dogs never stood still, made picking them out for a shot next to impossible.

Looking down the trail, the brothers saw the rope bridge for the first time. Standing taut and less than fifty yards away, the simple, twine-and-board bridge strung across an opening in the island's cliff side. Anchored to massive elm trees on each side, Tomek and Drake continued to walk backwards to it, arrows nocked and ready to shoot should the spotted dogs decide that twin was on their menu that night.

Once reaching the edge of the bridge, it was quite clear that, safe or not, they would be crossing it in order to place the massive gorge between them and the laughing beasts that once again had packed up and materialized from inside the ferns.

The sounds of the hoots soon were coming from every direction, and it seemed as if the twins were completely surrounded. Every few seconds, a hyena would burst out of the ferns on one side of the road and cross it in a dash, causing each of the boys to quickly draw and loose arrows, to no avail. After sending multiple arrows into the ferns unsuccessfully, it was clear than a new tactic would need to be employed.

"Save your arrows until they are closer and attack," Tomek suggested.

What once was a pack of seven had now doubled in numbers it seemed to the twins as they took their first step onto the dry, rotted boards that made up the bridge's foundation.

"Do you think they wanted us on the bridge?" Drake asked.

"What do you mean?" Tomek responded, not sure what his brother was referring to.

"Just seems like we're being herded here," Drake said.

Tomek leaned in closer, as the boys had paused four boards onto the bridge. With their feet now completely off the ledge, it meant that the bridge was now supporting their entire weight. While the bridge creaked and moaned from the stress of their combined weight, it held.

"No other choice," replied Tomek. "Last I checked, we didn't have wings to fly across this gorge, and at the end of it was that bog. I'll take my chance on the bridge rather than try to outrun a pack of hyenas through a bog."

"Good point," Drake said as they now stood at the halfway point of the bridge, still slowly moving one board at a time as the bridge swayed in the wind that was now picking up beach sand and swirling to an almost violent proportion.

Looking back at the pack of hyenas, the twins could clearly see the black spots that sat upon their tan hides as the longer fur along their spines stood up in a menacing, hump-back manner. The dogs paced back and forth along the edge of the gorge just up from the entrance boards of the bridge but did not attempt to cross or enter the bridge in any way. It was as if there was an invisible line that stopped them from entering, and the twins were happy for the hyenas' lack of intestinal fortitude when it came to what must have seemed to them like walking on air. As quickly as the pack had grown, it vanished back into the ferns, leaving only three beasts at the opening the twins had originally used to get on the bridge.

While not being able to see the hyenas, it was clear by their constant chorus of yelps, growls, and cackles that they were still in the area, although the majority of their sounds now echoed into the cavernous drop off below the twins as if it was coming from near the swamp. The thunder and the hyenas were having a competition to see who could make the most noise, and with the storm now upon them, thunder was winning the battle.

"They are going around," Drake yelled, worried that the dogs would soon occupy both sides of the bridge.

"We have to cross and find a pinch point," Tomek yelled as he began quickly stepping across the rickety boards remaining between them and the opposite side where the three, sentry hyenas still awaited the twins' retreat should they attempt to do so.

"Pinch point?" Drake replied, trying to keep up with the brother in front of him who was shaking the bridge in his wake and making it hard to do so.

Reaching the far side and getting their feet back on solid ground, they quickly took a survey of their surrounding area as the unrelenting cackles and screams of the hell beasts sounded. Unsure of their exact location, the twins figured the hyenas had made it through the bogs with ease and were now bearing down on their position.

"Pinch point?" Drake asked again.

"Yea, like Thermopolis," Tomek responded, impressing his brother in the moment by referencing the famous Greek battle of the three hundred.

Drake's moment of clarity regarding his brother's attention span during the history portion of Uncle's lessons was quickly ended as the rain began to fall. The sky opened up and began to violently soak all that was below. It was as if Mother Nature had finally decided to weep with shame for all she had put the boys through during their short but tremulous time here on the island.

"If the hyenas don't kill us, this lightning will," Drake yelled to Tomek, trying to talk above the deafening sounds of the storm's fury. Between the roar of the wind, the heavy rainfall, thunder, and lightning, Tomek barley heard what he said. Not being able to hear each other also meant not being able to hear the hyenas.

"Let's run to the edge," Tomek yelled.

"Why?" Drake asked.

"At least there they can't sneak up from behind us."

While Drake was normally the plan maker, he knew that Tomek always reacted well in emergency, combat, life-and-death situations, and he was happy to follow the lead. Agreeing that his edge strategy was their best option made it easier for him to let go of the situational reins as well.

Working their way to the far north end of the island in the storm would have been difficult on its own. However, the never-ending presence of the hyenas was not doing the twins any favors. Reaching the edge did mean the hyenas would have to attack from the front. Yet, unknown to the twins until they arrived at this particular cliff edge, the designers of the island had provided them with one, huge advantage in their struggle to survive the biting onslaught of the approaching hyenas: shelter.

Drake pointed to their left, as he was the first to see the tin roof as it was illuminated in a bolt of nearby lightning. Tomek looked, and without a word, they both began to sprint for the small shack that looked like it belonged more in the Shire of one of Uncle's books about Middle Earth than it did here on Ascension Island.

As they ran for it, they could see it had been constructed from the same, perfectly round, rock formations that were in the interior woods of the island. The rounded, stone balls deflected the wind, as it had nothing solid to impact, and flowed directly around the curved edges of the shed-like storage shelter. The circular design was the key to a structure surviving these types of winds for so many years.

Looking behind him as Drake closed the metal door, his adrenaline spiked as unknown to him, a hyena had charged and was less than a foot away. Jaws open and surging through the air, he could smell the rancid breath of the beast that it seemed had eaten nothing but rotten flesh its entire life.

Tomek reached around, slamming the door shut on the ribcage of the creature which was now half way inside the hut. Snapping and snarling, there was now no longer anything that resembled laughter about this hyena. It was there to kill, to kill and eat.

Tomek held the door shut, trapping the hyena's body half in and half out. Drake quickly drew his bow and sent an arrow just past the jaw of the beast, where it sliced down into the neck, through the heart, and exited out the bottom of the dog's abdomen. The wretched hound immediately backed up out of the door and began spinning in circles, spewing blood from its wounds as if it was trying to paint the surrounding ground to let the rest of the pack know exactly where its murderers were in hiding.

Tomek slammed the door, sliding the locking pin into position. Cold, wet, and happy to be alive, the boys just began to laugh. Uncontrollable, deep, guttural, belly laughs exploded from them both. The insanity of their situation was more than most could handle as they sat there in complete darkness, disbelieving that this was their new life.

As the rain mercilessly pounded the tin roof, the brothers' laughing stopped just in time to hear the hyenas pick it up. The chorus of bellowing, demonic wolves was clearly going to continue nonstop throughout the night. Tomek and Drake agreed that tomorrow they would have to deal with the dogs, but tonight, tonight they would sleep. Safely in their round rock shack, the boys lay down, and not even the mourning cries of the hyena pack for their fallen brethren would keep either twin from a solid night of sleep.

Lying there, slumped up against the walls, Tomek reached out in the dark and tapped his brother on the leg.

"What?" Drake said, annoyed at being woken up as he was drifting away into dream land.

"Did you hear about the hyena that got a job on Wall Street?" Tomek asked.

"No," Drake replied.

"Turns out he was a laughing stock."

Tomek proudly snickered, and at that very moment, Drake considered opening the door to throw his brother's ass out with the dogs in hopes that perhaps they might find his brand of comedy hilarious.

Drake just rolled over, took a deep breath, and said, "Good night."

12 HISTORY

"What is the list you guys were talking about?" Tony's questions had been non-stop since he learned of his father's true intentions regarding the hunt of a man he had come to like.

"It's like the score card, I guess," Garran answered while steering the boat out of the Grand Traverse Bay as they left port en route to Ascension Island. "It is not for bragging rights, however. It more so pays homage and respect to those who have fallen on the island."

"Oaky, so you keep score. So, do you give out points or something?" Tony asked.

"No, not exactly," his father replied.

"I'm confused." Tony's statement was obvious to his father.

"Look, I know you have lots of questions, and there will be time once we get to camp to go over a lot of this stuff," Garran said, trying to squash the conversation with his son.

"I just need to know some things," Tony continued.

"Like what?" Greggor asked, interrupting and interjecting himself into the conversation as he stepped into the room.

"He wants to know what we meant by the list and the book," Barr said, filling in Greggor with the details of their conversation so far.

"It's pretty simple, Tony," Greggor said as he sat down and kicked his legs up near the instrument panel, which quickly drew a stern eye from Barr. Stern enough that the eldest Stratton brother got the message and removed them, placing his feet back on the floor. Greggor leaned towards Tony, placed his hand on the boy's shoulder, and after looking around to make sure they were alone, lowered his voice and said, "When we get there, we will ditch Archer and give him a head start. This makes it more challenging, and after all, that is the entire point. The challenge."

"Then what?" Tony asked,

"We head to our cabin, which is like our home base. It is safe there. Archer won't know where it is, and it wouldn't matter if he did, because it is protected from intruders."

"Protected?"

"Yea, there is a big-ass wall and a couple of gates, but don't worry about that. You will see it when we get there. The first night, we will eat, drink, and laugh. We will get the book out and go over the list of names," Greggor explained.

"So, the list is all the hunters you guys have taken over the years?" Tony asked, thinking he was starting to catch on.

"Not the hunters," his father said. "The hunted."

"Not exactly even that. Sometimes it is both," Greggor admitted.

"Huh?" Tony asked.

"If your name is on the list, it means you died on the island. There is a lot of shit out there that can and will kill a man other than us. Not every name was some stranger we hunted. We have friends on the list. We have family on the list. But most importantly, we will keep you off that list," said Greggor, trying to settle the raging fear and uncertainty that must have been swelling inside the young mind of Tony.

"I think keeping me off the list is a great idea," Tony said with a smile, cracking a small joke in order to relieve some of the tension.

Garran Barr could see a bit of unearned confidence growing in his son's eye and wanted to make sure he fully grasped the weight of the situation they would be facing.

"You see, son, to survive on Ascension Island, a deer knows that every day he needs to run faster than the fastest lion. And every day, the lion knows that he needs to run faster than the slowest deer."

"Makes sense," Tony said.

"The point is, on Ascension, it does not matter if you are a deer or a lion. Either way, you better be running."

Tony's newfound confidence returned to a shaken status as he asked, "Has anyone ever escaped?"

"Escaped, no," Greggor said as he reentered the conversation.

"What does that mean?" Tony replied, sensing the hesitation in Greggor's answer.

Greggor again spoke up. "Years ago, when your father and I were on our very first Ascension Island hunt with your grandfather, we lost the target."

"Lost him?"

"Yea. He just vanished into the woods. We had figured that one of the beasts had got him or that he tried to make a swim for it or something," Greggor explained.

"The guy was a ghost, and that's what we call him. So, no, his real name—Tom—does not appear on the list. He was some kind of a military survival instructor, and it is because of him that your grandfather's name is on the list. He was the kind of guy that could have lived in the woods on his own for years. They should have known better," Barr said, revealing to his son that his own grandfather had been murdered on the island.

"What?" Tony exclaimed. "Grandpa had a heart attack while fishing."

"That's what we told you, of course," Barr said coldly to his son.

Greggor placed his hand on the boy's shoulder and settled him down. "The truth hurts sometimes, young man, but your Grandpa went down fighting."

Garran then walked over to the small table where the other two sat and explained, "See, son, your grandfather and his pals would just grab anyone off the street, bring them out here, and hunt them down. They did zero research, and to them it was a numbers game. We are different. This is about the hunt and about the challenge. That is why guys like Archer are researched and only then selected. We need the challenge, but want to keep our names off the list at the same time. When the old guys picked up that Tom character, they had never met him. They knew he had a twin brother back in Pine Run at some podunk store and that was it. Their mistake put four names on the list that trip. Four names that were not 'Tom.' And the truth is, mine and Greggor's name should be there too, but he just vanished. Like a ghost in the wind, he was gone."

"Do you think he is still out there, like, out there living on the island?" Tony asked, showing that he was starting to get worried.

"No, this was years ago. We have never seen a track or trace of him at all," Greggor said. "The ghost just vanished."

Tony stood up, placing his hands atop the control panel as he stared out into the horizon of blue water. "I just have one more question then, I guess."

"Okay," his dad said.

"So, why even keep the list?" Tony asked, looking at Garran.

His father walked over to him and sighed. "It reminds us that this is not a game and anyone that we bring here, can be a ghost."

13 TWO DOORS

The rhythmic thumping sound of the chopper's rotating blades was quite the wakeup call for the twins. Jumping up and scurrying to the side walls, Tomek and Drake peered through the spaces between rounded wall rocks. The reverberated echo of the chopper made it seem like it was even louder inside their shelter than any helicopter they were accustomed to hearing before.

"Where the hell is that coming from?" Tomek asked.

"No clue. We should have heard it from miles away," Drake replied.

Neither twin would have ever imagined that the Barr's aerial equipment would have been launched from atop their luxury yacht. The *Full Coverage* had pulled into the island's north side, inlet harbor silently overnight and anchored just inside the break wall, safe from the waves but still almost two hundred yards from the island's shoreline. Getting closer was impossible without destroying the boat.

The particular spot where the boat rested was the only place near the island that offered safe harbor via air as well as being secure from the unpredictable swells that called this part of Lake Michigan home. So it was there that the hunting party loaded into the helicopter and quickly covered the two football fields of length in order to now be hovering above Ascension Island.

The aircraft continued past the twins and stopped to hover over a small section of the meadow just west of their shack.

"What are they doing?" Tomek asked. "And who are they?"

Drake was unsure, but he knew that his brother's second question was more important than the first. "No idea. Maybe they are trying to scare away the lion?" he guessed.

"I killed the lion," Tomek reminded his brother.

"They don't know that, jackass."

"Good point," Tomek admitted.

Sliding the latch on the rock shelter's door, Tomek slowly began to open it.

"What are you doing?" Drake scolded.

"Listen, if that thing scares a lion away, I am sure the hyenas are long gone," Tomek said confidently. "And if they do land, this shelter might be the first thing they come check. I don't—we don't know who the hell is in that thing or how they snuck up on us. We should move through the woods and the fields, out of sight, and watch them. Agreed?" Tomek asked, but his brother knew there really was no disagreeing.

"Got it," Drake said as he followed his twin out into the thin line of hardwoods that scuttled around the edge of the drop-off overlooking the bay. Taking a full inventory of their surroundings, while keeping eyes out for lions, bears, and hyenas, Drake grabbed Tomek's shoulder and pointed down into the lake below.

"That explains it," Tomek said as he saw the *Full Coverage* anchored way off the island below. "Think it is Annette?"

"I don't know. I mean, she could fly an airplane, so who knows?" Drake admitted to not having a clue.

The debating of who it was hovering over their island would not last very long due to the fact that the helicopter was now losing altitude and clearly intending to land in the dry spot of the meadow where the grasses were shortest. Drake and Tomek moved quickly into position, utilizing the propeller's violent washing of the taller grasses and bushes to hide their approach. Once in position on the outskirts of the opening, the twins remained there, lying prone in the grass much like a lion ready to pounce, as they observed the far side, rear passenger door open. Falling out of the chopper just as it landed was a bloody and beaten man of what the twins considered to be a large size. Archer rolled away from the flank of the aircraft as all three Stratton brothers stepped out, joining him on the meadow floor. Within thirty yards of the landing zone, they could clearly over hear the conversation.

"Aw, what's a matter, Archer?" Ricardo asked, leaning over the man who was now curled up in ball.

"Get up, you fucking pussy," Sven demanded, grabbing Archer by the back of his ponytail and forcing him to his feet. Once standing, Archer was quickly dropped back to the ground in a sack of pain thanks to Greggor's right fist impacting his unprotected stomach.

"You guys are fucking crazy," Archer shouted through broken teeth, busted lips, and bleeding gums.

Sitting in the dual cockpit, Garran looked over to Tony and said, "This is not the beginning of the end for good ol' Archer, son. This is the end of his beginning."

"Huh?" Tony said.

"Archer is no longer a free man, no longer a man at all. Archer is a beast, a beast that must be vanquished. He belongs to the island. He is an animal. He is a beast. Ascension Island is the home of many beasts, and now Archer has joined their ranks," Garran said, attempting to be philosophical with his son, who was still struggling to take in the gravity of the situation.

"What the fuck? You brought me out here just to beat the shit out of me?" Archer asked, again struggling to speak through the pain while gasping at air.

"Yup. Well, more or less," Sven said, laughing as he kicked the crawling man in the backside of his ass in an attempt to embarrass him more than injure.

Ricardo knelt down, getting face to face with the man-beast, lifted Archer's chin, and said, "You see, Archer, we all are going have a little adventure come tomorrow morning. You are now our prey. But don't worry. We are going to give you one whole day to get settled, and then—well, it's on."

"What's on?" Archer asked.

"The hunt," Sven yelled this time as he kicked Archer's rib cage again, dropping him to the ground.

A puff of dry, meadow dirt went air born as he slammed down and rolled over. Picking the beaten man up by his hair again, Greggor got Archer to his feet.

"Take this. You may need it."

Greggor handed Archer a small, folding, Buck knife.

"Thanks, but just so you know, I am going to kill you with it," Archer said, turning his head and spitting a mouthful of blood into the face and neck of Greggor, coving him in a patch of red DNA.

"That's the spirit," Greggor said as he laughed manically and looked to the left and right at each of his brothers.

The ongoing conversation was interrupted by the sound of the helicopter's engine twirl firing up as the blades began to slowly rotate.

"Guess the boss man has had enough," Ricardo said as he sucker punched Archer directly in his left temple and knocked him down to the ground. The still folded Buck knife flung into the air, landing only a few feet away from the twins as they remained motionless in the taller grass.

Greggor and Ricardo climbed into the cabin of the chopper as Sven took a knee next to the barely conscious piece of meat they once called Archer.

"You got two options, buddy, two doors to walk through, if you may:

You lay here and die, or you fight and die."

"Thanks for the heads up," Archer grumbled, spitting more blood on the ground.

Sven patted him on the back of his head like he was comforting a small child and said, "There's a shit storm behind door one and a storm of shit behind door two. I don't care what door you choose to open. Either way, it is storming, and I'm going to be the one inside that door. And you—you are a dead motha fucka."

Sven completed his threatening point by pushing Archer's face down into the dirt of the meadow's floor as he got up to walk back to his ride, which would soon be airborne.

Rambling back to the chopper which was now ready to lift from the ground, Sven looked up to see his eldest brother Greggor yelling something at him that was lost in sound of the helicopter's whirling rotors and revved up engine. Looking at his brother, Sven lifted his hand up to his ear, signaling that he had no clue what Greggor was saying. Sven looked into the passenger side cockpit to see Tony Barr pointing behind him towards the spot where Archer was lying. Sven drastically spun around, expecting to see one of the island's animals already pouncing towards their weakened target. Only there was no animal or beast behind him. There was nothing.

Standing at the edge of the fuselage, Sven yelled into the open door, "Where did he go?"

Ricardo yelled back, "Just got up and ran into the bush."

What a sissy, Sven thought to himself as he lifted his left leg into the chopper as the landing skids awkwardly lifted off the ground. Sitting halfway in the chopper, Sven hung outside of the main compartment much like a Vietnam War-era gunner. Looking inside at his two brothers, Sven began to shrug his shoulders and was about to lament his thoughts on Archer's character to them when his words were choked back by a rushing pain in his right leg.

Archer had charged from out of the tall grass that he had originally retreated to, slamming all four inches of the Buck knife blade into the youngest Stratton brother's calf. Sven's scream, combined with Archer's weight on the skid, made Garran temporarily lose control of the bird as it lunged to the left, violently throwing both Archer and Sven from the skid and into the air, slamming them back down to the meadow's ground floor.

With multiple alarm whistles chattering and interior gauge lights flashing, Garran wasn't able to gain control of the helicopter's horizontal spin enough to set it back down on the ground in an orderly, landing fashion. In a somewhat wild, spinning motion, the chopper bounced up and off the ground, only gaining a foot of altitude before slamming back down into the dirt. Garran slammed the controls back and forth as the aircraft began to spin raucously as if it was a merry-go-round on a schoolyard playground.

Sven quickly found his way on top of Archer and began to strike him wildly upon his head and chest. Sitting on top of the man, Sven had taken position much like a mixed martial artist would in a cage fight to the death. Archer attempted to cover his face and neck, redirecting the blows one by one as he also struggled to find the knife he had lost yet again as he was thrown to the ground. Archer realized the last time he had the blade it was four inches deep in Sven's leg.

Punch after punch found its mark, and just as Archer felt himself about to black out, the punches just stopped. Sven's body went limp, falling motionless to his side. The limpness of Sven's body was preceded by an odd sound that seemed to briefly silence the roar and wind of the helicopter's blades. Looking over at his opponent's body, it was quite clear as to what had saved him.

Archer couldn't help but to laugh to himself as he looked upon Sven's face. There was nothing in particular on Sven's face that he found amusing.

It was not what was on his face that made Archer laugh. It was what was not on his face that did.

Sven's face lay there on the meadow ground to Archer's left. And his body lay to the right. The hunter's face had been completely removed in one, perfect, vertical slice of the twirling rear rotor blade of Garran Barr's helicopter. The blade had struck the Stratton brother right below the chin, violently lacerating its way up through the jaw, past the nasal cavity and the frontal lobe of his brain, on its way out through the top of the skull.

While the faceless body lay motionless, Archer's laughs stopped as he quickly gazed into the eyes of his dead captor. Empty and lifeless, removed from the head they once belonged to, Sven's eyes moved back and forth as if they were searching for an answer. His pupils shot up towards the sky as the last nerves refusing to die continued to blink. Sven's last sight was of the helicopter leaving him behind.

"Holy Christ, that was close," Garran said, pulling back on the yoke and gaining altitude as Ricardo and Greggor looked down in disbelief and anger over the quick death of their youngest brother.

"Dad, I want to go home," Tony said, second guessing their entire reason for coming to Ascension Island in the first place. For now, it was clear that death was a real possibility here.

"No," Garran said, looking at his son sternly. "We are going to kill that Archer bastard and put his name on the list right after Sven's."

The twins watched as the chopper gained altitude and flew straight south, where they were able to see it dip below the island's horizon and drop into the bowl that housed their cabin. With their eyes so fixated on the helicopter, they both had paid no attention to their surroundings or the whereabouts of Archer. Both were surprised to find him completely gone from the area as their attention returned to the battle arena before them.

14 CAMP

With the helicopter now grounded in the garden area of the cabin, it was clear to the hunters that someone had been there prior to their arrival. The twins' fire had been extinguished fully by the torrential downpour of the previous night's storm, yet the stacked wood and charred remains of their partially burnt logs was evidence enough to Barr that someone had not only been there but been there recently. The most important thought to him was not just that someone had visited their cabin recently, but who it was weighed heavily on his mind.

As he stepped into the front breezeway door with his pistol drawn, Ricardo and Greggor followed close behind. Tony remained just outside the front door and would be the last one to enter, a position he was happy to take. All four men swept through the cabin's rooms, tactically clearing them of any danger while surveying the activity of whomever it was that had been there recently.

Garran was happy to find the cabin's rooms empty. A sentiment he did not carry over to the condition of the safe.

"What the fuck?" Ricardo said upon entering the small side room that housed the now empty safe.

"What was in there?" asked Tony.

"Just some old bows, arrows, and food," Garran replied to his son.

"Then what is the big deal?" Tony replied.

Garran shut the safe door and walked back out to the kitchen table and picked up the book of names from where Drake had left it sitting earlier the day before. "The fact that the bows are gone is not that big of a deal. We brought plenty of firepower for the hunt. The issue is not that the safe is empty. The issue is that the safe was opened at all."

"Did you lock it last year when we left?" Ricardo asked Barr.

Garran did not verbally answer his fellow hunter but shot him with a deep enough glare that everyone in the room knew damn well the safe was secured prior to them leaving the island last time.

"Who all has the code?" Tony asked, continuing to grasp at what exactly was going through his father's head.

"Who has the code that is still alive?" Ricardo butted in. "Only the three of us and your dad."

"Three of us?" Tony asked. "No one told me the code."

Ricardo realized that he had accounted for his recently faceless brother when he made his count and recanted. "The two of us and your dad, I mean."

"No, there could be more." Garran said.

"Those old-timers are long dead," Greggor replied, joining the conversation.

Garran agreed but was unsure, stating, "Yea, they are, but who knows who they may have told."

"Good point," Greggor said.

Ricardo sat down, rubbing his head. "Old-timers get a little loopy on their deathbed sometimes. Hell, one of them probably drew someone a map on how to get here and everything."

"Yep. Could be anyone on this island with us at this point, I guess," Garran warned his fellow hunters in a serious tone.

"Sweet, more names to add to the list," Ricardo joked.

"Think Archer somehow knew one of the old-timers and got into the safe?" Tony pondered out loud.

Garran shook his head. "Doubt it. Plus, no way would he get here before us being that we were in a helicopter."

"Yea, that's true," said Tony, feeling stupid for having asked what he now knew was a dumb question.

Garran then opened the red book in his hand and looked through the pages full of names. Stopping on the last page that they had left off on, he set the book on the table and pointed to the first empty line available.

"Speaking of the list."

Greggor stepped up, grabbed the book from Barr, and used one of the pens from the crystal bowl in the middle of the table to fill out the latest casualty information. His hand was shaking as he wrote his fallen brother's name. Tony silently wondered if his hand was shaking due to grief, anger, nerves, or a combination of all three.

The four hunters exited the small cabin, walked back towards the garden area that served as the makeshift helipad, and began to unload their equipment. A small armory had been stashed in the small cargo hold of the aircraft. Gun case after gun case was pulled out and placed in a pile next to the cabin. A few cases of kitchen and food supplies made the pile grow, with gear and clothing bags rounding out the pile.

A rifle, shotgun, and various handguns were each brought along by each hunter, and it was clear to Tony that what his dad had said about the missing bows not being that big of a deal was very true. The men and Tony were going to war, and they were prepared to do so.

Looking down at the pile of gear, Tony bent down to pick up a bag and carry it into the cabin but stopped upon seeing something he had only seen in movies or videogames strapped to the bag's handle.

"Is this what I think it is?"

"Hell, yes, it is," Greggor replied.

Tony shook his head in disbelief. "You brought a freaking grenade?"

"Damn straight. Only got one, though, so don't go playing around with it," replied Greggor as he took the bag out of Tony's hand and headed into the bunk room with it.

Tony was amazed at the green, baseball-sized explosive device.

"How did you get it?"

Greggor looked at the young man and began to laugh. "My daddy brought home an entire case of these here MK2s from Vietnam. Hell, we blew most of them up playing around as kids, but this is the last one left. I am going to shove it up Archer's ass and watch his balls shoot out his eye sockets in honor of Sven."

Tony laughed at the violent notion briefly before realizing Greggor was not joking. Lowering his eyes to the ground in shame, his conscience quickly reminded him that murder was no laughing matter. Whether it is by bow, gun, chopper blade, or a grenade up the ass, murder was murder. And murder was not an atrocity he was sure his mind would let him commit. Yet for now, the son of Garran Barr decided it was best to keep quiet and go with the flow. Tony figured with this much firepower, it would not take long to hunt down and kill Archer. The sooner Archer was dead, the sooner they would get to return home.

It took less than an hour to have the gear unloaded and weapons staged for the rest of their week-long planned hunt. The party joined up again inside the cabin. Greggor slumped in the corner and sharpened his large, axe blades, while Ricardo stood over the gas range where he began to prepare the traditional first meal at camp, which traditionally consisted of fried bologna sandwiches.

With Sven's name now clearly and officially added to the list of those who fell to the dangers of time spent on Ascension Island, Greggor glanced down at the open book and couldn't help but notice the name at the top of the page. Pointing at it and leaving his finger on the page, he made eye contact with the others in the room.

"Think he is still here?"

"Who? The ghost?" Garran said with a rolling of his eyes.

"Could be. We never found his body, and he killed just about every one of us that year," Ricardo added.

Garran rolled his eyes again. "You Stratton boys sure do like to let your imaginations get on a roll."

"So, you really don't know if he is dead?" Tony asked.

"Everyone on the list died on this island, son, but the island has a way of taking what and who it wants. Everyone on the list, rest assured, is dead," he said, answering his son with confidence.

"Except the ghost," Greggor again claimed.

Tony looked at his dad. "Yea. What about the ghost?"

Ricardo placed his hand on Tony's shoulder as he walked up to the table. All four of them were now looking down at the table, focusing on the name written at the top of the same page that held Sven's.

"The ghost was impossible to kill. He moved in the shadows and toyed with us the entire time while picking off your grandfather and his friends one by one. He set traps and was always one, if not two steps ahead. It was like fighting a demon. Every time I turned around, there was another dead body."

"How did you survive?" Tony prodded.

"We got back to the helicopter and left, but really I think he simply spared us, I guess," Garran explained.

Tony was still confused. "And if you didn't kill him, why is he on the list?"

"We got off the island, and when we came back, we never found his body or even a trace of him," Garran said.

"So, he could have escaped? Or he could still be out here?"

Greggor confidently spoke up, "I highly doubt it. I did manage to put an arrow into his leg. We figured a lion or bear did the rest of the job for us. So that's why his name is on the list."

Garran grabbed a glass from the interior pine cupboards and poured himself a glass of water from the sink. Sitting down at the table, he leaned his chair back on two legs as he stretched out his own.

"Someone is on this island with us, boys. It ain't no ghost. That's for sure."

The remaining Stratton brothers joined Garran at the table, after obtaining their own drinks, and agreed with him that the notion of the ghost being around after all these years was just silly.

"So, what now? We just sit around?" Tony asked, showing his uncomfortable impatience.

Garran Barr raised his glass of water as if it was a monarch's goblet of wine and he was making a royal toast.

"Tonight we dine, my son. We feast like kings, and in the morning, we hunt."

Raising their glasses, they all joined in and went along with the toast.

"To Sven," Ricardo said.

"To Sven," the group replied.

Garran stood up as the room again fell silent and used the moment to warn the group that not only included his lifelong friends but now his only son.

"Men, Sven's death is not the beginning of the end. It is the end of the beginning. Time to do what we do best."

Tony had heard his father say those same words about Archer just hours ago, but he didn't feel the need to let the others know about his father's lack of originality.

Raising his voice at the end of the short speech led the group into an obnoxious roar as each of them grabbed their helping of food from the kitchen and sat down at the large, rectangular table that was much too fancy for this type of cabin.

The older men continued to talk about the glory days of hunts gone by and share funny stories of their fallen brother. Tony was disturbed by the crass and almost uncaring nature of both Greggor and Ricardo. He did not understand how they were not grieving, as he felt would be appropriate, a mere three hours after watching their youngest brother horrifically killed. Nonetheless, he looked through the book and stared at a name near the top of the page, the name that belonged to the so-called "Ghost" of Ascension Island.

Tom H. ~ The Ghost

15 AXE

As the slow moving hours passed around the camp and a late afternoon meal ended, Tony grew impatient and wanted to know more about the island. The youngest member of the hunting party was relieved to see his father and the men he considered his own uncles now checking their weapons and preparing for what he guessed would be an evening hunt.

"So, is it like hunting deer?" Tony asked. "Do we only go out in the morning and before dark?"

"Nah. We come and go as we please when we are hunting fools like Archer," Ricardo answered.

"Once he is dead, we will spend the rest of the week hunting in a more traditional sense. The animals move when the sun is low, but we are hunting a man. A man does not always play by the rules of the animals," Greggor added.

Garran walked into the room in full camouflage, with his face painted in stripes of green and black war paint. This was certainly a look his son had never seen him take on before. With a shotgun in his hands and pistols housed in tactical holsters on both thighs, Tony thought his father looked downright badass. A bandolier of shotgun ammo rounded out the leader of the group's arsenal. It was at this moment that Tony began to look over his own gear, which consisted of his deer hunting BAR .308 rifle and a single box of shells. Even though the rifle had been passed down to him by his dad, he still began to worry and felt under prepared.

Making Tony feel even less ready to hunt his fellow man, Greggor looked like a medieval knight in jet-black armor. The hunting gear and outfit of the eldest Stratton brother could not have been any different than that of Garran's. Black elbow braces, gloves, and shin guards that extended into knee pads made Greggor appear as if he was ready to go fight rioters in a protest.

While it certainly was not traditional hunting gear, it was perfect for killing and defending against the attack of another person.

The only thing more peculiar than Greggor's choice of black armor was the weaponry that adorned his body. The green grenade that Tony had noticed earlier now dangled off the side plate of Greggor's thick, plastic chest plate. As Greggor turned around, Tony noticed a set of twin battle axes mounted across the man's back in an X-formation. The carbon fiber-wrapped handles looked to be as sleek and strong as the silver head with its razor-sharp edges. The edges of each blade actually glinted in the light as they deflected a bright spot onto the ceiling of the small room as he moved about.

"Really? Axes again this year?" Ricardo asked.

"Hell, yea," his brother answered enthusiastically.

"Okay, um, why axes?" Tony asked.

However, before Greggor could answer, Ricardo piped in with a barrage of insults and jokes.

"You see, young blood, he brings the axes every year 'cause—well, quite frankly—he never gets the kill, and someone has to chop wood."

Garran jumped in on the fun, adding, "You look like the offspring of a gay ninja that broke into a cave and accidentally got a dwarf's wife knocked up."

Everyone was laughing at this point. Greggor was able to take the jokes, and even Tony began to smile.

"Well, then, ninjas are badass, and dwarves are as strong as rocks," Greggor said as he removed one of his axes from the back scabbard and began to shave whiskers off of his face with it.

"Strong as a rock, huh?" Tony asked.

"Yes, sir," Greggor nodded.

"Smart as one, too, then, huh?" Tony joked as he sat down on the floor, causing his father and the remaining Stratton brother to erupt in sidesplitting laughter. Only this time, it was clear that the humor had not been appreciated by Greggor.

Greggor stopped his shave, checking his face in the glassy, metallic reflection of his blade's head, and flipped the axe around as if he was going to slide it into the holder. Tony looked away for a split second, noticing a fish jumping on the lake out of the dining room window of the cabin. Glancing back, he froze in his place as the loud thud of the axe's head impacted the cabin's oak flooring and lodged in place. A mere two inches away from the one piece of his body all men appreciate most was a razor's edge that had been thrown with such force and accuracy that, as it passed between both Ricardo and Garran, the only sound was a slight *whoosh* as the blade and handle turned end over end.

Tony looked down, and then looked up, and then looked down yet again as the cabin was now silent. Tony now knew why Greggor had chosen to carry the axes and was at a loss for words as he inched his crotch back and away from the blade that again glinted in the light.

Garran Barr, while being slightly amused in the situation, was not overly excited at the fact that his best friend had just launched an axe at his son's balls. Yet he knew that if Greggor had wanted to hurt Tony, he would have, and this was just a perfect example of Greggor being Greggor.

Tony stood up and grabbed the axe, struggling to pull it out of the floor, a task which he did not want to let the others know was difficult for him. Tony handed the double-bladed, dwarf's weapon back to Greggor and said, "I sure am glad you didn't throw the grenade at me."

Again, the room fell to laughter as Greggor joined back in the lighthearted frolic of emotions. Breaking up the ball-busting, Garran pulled the slide back on one of his Glocks, loading a shell into the chamber as he motioned to the front screen door.

"Well, let's get to it."

Nodding in agreement, Greggor and Ricardo stepped out of the cabin as Tony followed, closing the door behind them.

Standing in front of the massive, iron-clad door, the group stopped to discuss their tactical plan. Tony read the ominous message carved into the door and felt as uneasy as the twins did upon their first venture up the stairs of Ascension.

Garran pulled out a folded piece of paper from his inner breast pocket. To Tony's relief, it was a map of the island.

Garran then detailed his plan for the evening hunt. "Tony and I are going to head into the meadow up the west trail. I doubt Archer is still where we dropped him, but if he took the easy way out of the area, the meadow is where he will be. Plus, I want a shot at that lion I saw last year. I bet he is even bigger now."

"He ain't running out in the open, I bet. He is in the swamp, I am thinking. I'll head up the middle and walk the swamp up and around. You and your axes want to come with me, lumberjack?" Ricardo said.

"Nope. I will hunt the valley. That way, we have the whole damn place covered. One of us is bound to get a crack at him. That is, if the island herself has not already claimed him," Greggor said, detailing his plans for the evening.

"Very well, then," Barr said as he opened the heavy latch on the door and began the climb up to the hunting fields.

Walking step by step, climbing the carved rock stairwell, and looking up at Ricardo in front of him, Barr found an odd sense of satisfaction mixed with a splice of humor in the fact that Ricardo did not rely on multiple guns and especially no battle axes. The middle Stratton brother often served as the family and camp butcher on their trips. Just like any other butcher would have, Ricardo chose knives. Ricardo was a walking butcher shop, with knives on his hip, in his coat, and even tied into the laces of his boots. He did have an Armalite rifle, chambered in .223, slung over his back just in case, but if Ricardo was to get the kill, it would happen up close and personal and most likely with a blade.

Upon reaching the top, the group met up one last time, and all agreed to be back prior to dark. It was understood that after dark they would be on their own until the following morning. If for any reason they needed help, each hunter carried a signal flare gun. Simply shooting it into the air would in theory bring the others to their location. The idea of the flare guns was not always part of their arsenal. Each hunter carrying a flare became a necessary addition, thanks to The Ghost and his dismantling of their party years ago.

As discussed, the father-son, Barr combination worked left into the meadow, and Tony got his first real taste of the specialty that was Ascension as he saw numerous whitetails, mule deer, and even a warthog along the trail. It was clear to him that this was nothing like hunting in the comforts of the Michigan's Lower Peninsula.

The excitement of seeing the unfamiliar wild game was quelled as his father constantly reminded him, "This is not a tourist safari, son. Archer is the trophy."

Ricardo and his knives found the swamp wet and full of mosquitoes, thanks to the previous night's storm. He skirted the edge, keeping the hardwood bluff's elevation change to his advantage. Walking the tram road that sliced into the hillside meant he could be out of the swamp and its swarming army of bloodsucking insects but yet overlook it. Being in the timber and swamp meant less sunlight, and he would face darkness much quicker than the other hunters. Although darkness would not be an issue for Ricardo, being that his older brother would be the only hunter who would be in need of light.

Greggor had easily made his way through the south wall cliffs, enjoying the views they provided of the seemingly endless waters of the Great Lake.

Passing through the hardwood section of his path with about ninety minutes of daylight left, the axe-bearing brute was exiting the valley of the ferns when he caught movement ahead of him on the opposite side of the water inlet.

Ducking low, almost lying flat on his belly, he watched from across the gorge, about one hundred yards away, as Tomek and Drake arrived back at the round shelter. The sight of the twins was clearly a shock to the hunter. Upon first seeing movement, he expected it to be Archer or possibly even Tony and Garran making their way round the crest of the island's north end. However, seeing two teenagers carrying the bows that were originally secured in their safe back at the cabin was not what he expected. To Greggor, the lived-in and open condition of the cabin upon their arrival began to quickly make more sense.

As the twins entered the round rock structure to raid the work benches and shelving units inside for any possible supplies, Greggor made his move, jumping up and sprinting to the edge of the gorge. Standing with his back against the large oak tree that served as the tethering anchor for the suspended bridge, Greggor peered around the trunk and watched the twins. Pondering how they got on the island and who they were, he took a deep breath and reminded himself that it didn't really matter. They were on the island and were not part of his group. Therefore, their names belonged on the list.

With zero intention of crossing the rope bridge, due to his being a bit of a klutz and having a healthy fear of falling, Greggor remained hidden and laid in wait. As a heavy fog swelled in the bottom of the gorge, Greggor glanced down and was surprised to see that it was so thick below him the water was not visible. Knowing the twins only had a few options, Greggor was not going to rush the situation. He knew they would either go back the way they came in and would run into Garran and Tony, or the duo would come towards him and cross the bridge. The third option was that the twins could possibly hunker down and not exit the shelter. In which case, he would then wait until dark and send a flare in the air, calling for reinforcements.

Within a short, ten-minute wait, Greggor watched as the twins exited the shack. It was apparently clear that Greggor would not be using the signal flare after dark as the twins headed towards the rope bridge.

Tomek was the first twin to get onto the bridge as Greggor remained behind the tree. Using the combination of the trunk and the quickly building fog, the human hunter waited patiently for the perfect moment to make his presence known. He looked quickly around the tree once more, watching as Tomek had crossed the halfway point of the bridge's expanse, with Drake only a few steps behind. They were close enough now for him to hear their conversation.

"You think the helicopter landed at the cabin?" Tomek asked Drake.

"No idea, but I would guess so," Drake responded with uneasiness in his voice as the foot planks creaked like the old door of a dilapidated haunted house. "They just dropped that dude off. He kills one of them and then vanishes into the brush. What in the hell is going on here?"

"Kind of like the man-hunting story Uncle used to tell us when we were younger. Remember him talking about the snake killing the mice in the fog?" Tomek said.

He was referring to an old story they both knew well but had always considered fiction, not knowing that their very Uncle himself had spent time on their new island home.

"Of course I remember it," Drake said as his voice again trembled while the bridge swayed back and forth in an unpredictable manner.

Tomek smiled, turning around to look back at Drake.

"You okay, brother?"

Drake did not answer. He could not answer. Drake was frozen in place. Tomek probed at him with a list of questions. Each question remained unanswered, getting the same vacant response as the one before it.

"Cat got your tongue?"

"You this afraid of heights?"

"You didn't seem to mind it in the plane?"

"You see a ghost or something?"

"Hello…"

Tomek then saw in his twin's eyes what his mouth could not say. Jerking his head and body back around, Tomek laid his own eyes on exactly what Drake had been staring at over his shoulder, the very sight that had rendered him mute.

There, at the end of the bridge, standing on solid ground, was Greggor Stratton. The hunter had trapped them in the middle of a rope bridge in an eerie, intimidating fog. Overlooking a three-hundred-plus-foot fall, Greggor remained still, maintaining a devilish smile. While the twins could not see the rocks and water below, they knew they were there.

Greggor did not say a word as he raised his axe blade into the sky. In the brief moment that the blade remained at the apex of his swing, both twins headed in opposite directions. Tomek rushed towards the hunter as Drake awkwardly attempted to retreat to the far side of the bridge.

Neither twin reached their intended destination prior to the silver blade of Greggor's axe slamming down and slicing completely through the wrist-thick support rope. The bridge lurched to the side as Tomek fell, holding on to the one remaining solid rope. He looked back to where his brother had been and saw nothing on or near the bridge as the fog made it difficult to tell what remained.

Tomek panicked and yelled, "Drake!"

Greggor again sliced downward through the other guide rope, and the weight of the twins slunk the bridge downward. The entire structure now resembled the shape of a V. The bridge's structural integrity had briefly held as the ropes weaving through the boards held the floor intact. This allowed each twin to gain a few more feet of elevation as they grasped and climbed towards their respective sides. The middle point of the bridge's V quickly unhinged and loudly snapped as the bridge gave way, each half relinquishing to the gravity that pulled it down with a furious, descending vengeance.

16 FALLEN

Tomek grabbed on to the floor planks of the bridge as he fell. Closing his eyes as tight as they ever had been, he awaited the forced trauma that would rip apart his body as he abruptly landed upon the rocks. With his only hope being that perhaps he may find water and somehow survive, Tomek found it funny that he was able to think of these things as he fell to his death.

The arch of his descent changed unexpectedly as he felt a centrifugal force change his vertical fall into a horizontal swing. As brief as it was, he quickly knew what had happened while his body slammed into the rock wall, crushing his fingers between the wall and the back side of the boards he had his fingernails buried into. The side guide ropes had been sliced, causing the bridge to plummet once the middle section succumbed to their weight, but the floorboards where anchored into the rock ledge at each end as well. All that was hanging between Tomek and the solid ground above him was a bridge full of planks that had been transformed into a wobbling, thirty-foot, vertical ladder.

Kicking with his feet, Tomek found space between two of the planks and wedged his toes in between them, allowing him to stand on the top edge. Looking back to find his brother, the fog prevented him from seeing the other side.

Again, he yelled, "Drake, hold on and climb!"

Knowing he had not heard a large splash reverberate off the rock walls from below, there was no way that his twin had hit the water. That meant only one of two things. Either Drake was hanging from a section of the ladder on the other side of the gorge, or his lifeless body had hit the rocks below. With the fog now engulfing him fully, Tomek could verify neither prospect, and with Drake not answering his calls, he knew the worst of the two was more likely. Dangling from the rock wall, Tomek gathered his thoughts and knew that while he would grieve the loss of his brother, now was not the time.

With his mangled, bleeding, and cut up hands, Tomek climbed upward, step by step, and struggled to keep a grip on each plank as blood ran down his forearms and dripped off the end of his elbow. His only concern at this moment was reaching the top. There was no sadness, no anger, and no fear in his mind as he made progress up the wall.

Reach the top. Reach the fucking top, Tomek said to himself, repeating the mantra over and over in his mind as he gained elevation with each, excruciating step. Even if Greggor was at the top waiting for him, Tomek did not care. At least he would have made it to the top.

At the last step, Tomek blindly reached up and over the top ledge in a hopeless attempt at finding something to grasp and hold on to. Only four feet away from the end of his daunting climb for survival, Tomek pawed at the sandy, dirt floor, grabbing at the little patches of moss that sprouted from the ledge.

"Well, I'll be damned, son," Greggor remarked upon seeing the hand of Tomek breach the rock ledge.

Tomek was not shocked to hear the man's voice and felt anger growing inside him. After all, he had not liked the sheriff calling him 'son,' and this man standing above him on the solid ground was no exception to the rule.

Gritting his teeth, Tomek replied, "I am not your fucking son."

Ignoring the boy's comment, Greggor reached down, grabbed Tomek's hand, and in one, unrelenting, fluid motion, pulled and swung the twin up over the rock ledge, almost six feet over into the dirt, where Tomek rolled multiple times before coming to a stop.

Lying on his chest, Tomek raised his head, spat dirt out of his mouth, and pushed up with his arms. Exhaustion and fatigue had given way to a raging flow of lactic acid in his muscles as they succumbed to the weight of his own body. A single push-up was not only improbable but physically impossible. Tomek rolled to his hip, getting his feet under him, and labored as he got up onto one knee. Looking up at Greggor, who was now walking towards him with axe in hand, Tomek reached for the knife on his belt only to find that it was gone, most likely at the bottom of the ravine with his bow and his dead brother's body.

Tomek struggled to get his other foot up and under him, bracing his arms upon the rigid knee that had already made the journey. Stumbling to his feet, he weaved around and attempted to take a turning step to run from Greggor. But his legs gave way to the same weakness as his arms, and he slammed into the ground, breaking his fall with only his face. The impact of the ground on his head left him dizzied. Blinking furiously and shaking his head to make sense of his surroundings, Tomek felt a tremendous weight press upon his back as Greggor slammed his knees down along the spine, pinning the twin to the moss-covered ground under the large man's body mass.

As the plastic zip ties pulled tight against the bare skin of Tomek's wrists, he came to his senses enough to realize that he had, for all intents and purposes, been taken into custody.

Captured and cuffed, again, he thought, recollecting his time spent with Deputy Ravizza.

The plastic of the quickly applied riot restraints dug into his already bleeding hands, and he knew that asking for them to be loosened would be a waste of breath.

"You just may be my best trophy yet, son," Greggor said as he yanked up on Tomek's hands, lifting him off the ground and forcing the twin to his feet.

"I ain't your fucking son," Tomek reminded him. "And I sure as hell ain't no trophy, you murdering piece of shit."

"Now, now, son—I mean, boy—let's not pretend that had I let you and your little, African, tribal, look-alike spook cross this bridge that we would all be sitting here swapping hunting stories and sharing an ice cream cone," Greggor said as he pushed Tomek forward down the trail, spinning away from him to give himself a position behind Tomek.

Tomek knew that Greggor wanted him to walk down the path back through the valley of ferns, but he dragged his feet and resisted going along easily, secretly hoping the hyenas would show up and kill them both. Each time Tomek's uncooperativeness grew to an unacceptable level, it was met with a jab in the kidney delivered via the butt end of Greggor's axe handle.

Doubling over in pain, Tomek felt as if his insides erupted, though he did not fall. Regaining his breath and composure, he turned to look at his much larger capture and asked, "What are you doing on my island?"

"Your island?" Greggor laughed. "What in the hell makes you think this is your island?"

"I live here." Tomek's answer was simple and to the point.

"Not for long."

With Greggor's ominous reply, he began to think that he was not just under arrest, but that the consequences of his being caught on the bridge were soon to equal that of his twin brother, who was now lying dead at the bottom of the gorge. Walking forward slowly, with motivating pushes curtesy of the axe every so often, Tomek began to feel that falling would have been a better option, and he had never wished for a pine slider to hide in so bad in his life.

"Am I supposed to be scared?" Tomek asked.

"You are scared. I can tell," replied Greggor, who had placed his axe back into the sheath on his back. "But not as scared as that other one of ya was before he hit the rocks."

Tomek knew exactly what emotions Greggor was trying to evoke out of him and decided to fight back with words, keeping silent the building rage inside him at this point.

"You saw my brother's face before he died?" Tomek asked.

"Sure did. Looked like a little bitch."

"Well, I saw your brother's face after he died. That chopper sliced and diced him like a little—what did you say it was, again—oh yea, a little bitch."

Tomek's reply landed him square on the ground as the force of Greggor's boot in the small of his back crashed him downward. With his hands bound, he was unable to break the fall and felt his chest explode in pain as his clavicle made contact with the rocky terrain that formed this section between the ferns and hardwoods.

"How did you know he was my brother?" Greggor asked.

"Your boot just told me," Tomek replied, rolling over to his side in order to take the pressure of his own body weight off his chest.

"Get the fuck up on your feet and try to enjoy the rest of our walk, 'cause when we get back to camp, you are dead," Greggor threatened.

"I would say you could just kill me now, but today is not my day to die," Tomek said confidently.

"Is that so? And why is that?" Greggor chuckled as he opened the large, wooden door at the top of the Ascension steps.

Before Tomek thought about answering the brute's question, he again read the hand-carved lettering on the door's sign.

Welcome back from your attack.

For those who did not fall,

The hunt has changed you all.

For those who did not fall, he thought to himself, sad for the first time about the forlorn death of his twin. *Fucking nice. It's like they knew.*

He of course shook the thought out of his mind for the obvious reason that he had no idea who the *they* would be. Tomek decided that he was done playing the victim, and pine slider or not, it was time for him to get out of the restraints and somehow, some way, kill Greggor.

As they reached the bottom of the stairs and opened the large, wooden door, Tomek turned around. Looking Greggor in the eyes, he felt a bit of fury build within his soul.

"You know, there are only two days in a year when I can't kill you," Tomek said.

"I am not so easy to kill." Greggor smirked and pushed Tomek through the door, grabbing his shirt and guiding him towards the cabin. "Ok, I'll play your little game. What two days might they be?"

Tomek turned again, pulling away from Greggor's grip, and faced him.

"Yesterday, 'cause you hadn't invaded my home yet, my island yet."

"And the other?" Greggor said with a yawn.

"Tomorrow," Tomek scowled.

Greggor again laughed and sighed as if he was bored with the conversation.

"Well, I guess you are right. You couldn't kill me yesterday, and you won't be killing me tomorrow, because—"

Tomek interrupted, cutting him off mid-sentence.

"I can't kill you tomorrow, because I'm going to kill you today."

17 PRISONER

Tied to a large tulipwood tree near the fire pit, Tomek sat in silence as Greggor left him alone and went inside the cabin. Secured to the base of the tree's trunk around the waist and chest by a rope that had been wrapped around multiple times, his hands remained bound by the zip ties. Imprisoned up against the tree, Tomek thought he must look like one of the cartoon damsels in distress from the black-and-white cartoon videos they watched with Old Man Hawkins.

Looking down, he rolled his eyes and thought, *At least there is not a set of train tracks he can lay me down on.*

Looking around the cabin area, Tomek could see the helicopter sitting on its improvised landing pad of soft grass and multiple bags of gear set up against the front of the cabin and into the breezeway. He was surprised at how quickly the intruders had taken over their home and at the amount of things they had brought along. If he was somehow able to kill them all, their gear and supplies would come in handy for him and Drake.

"Drake," he said under his breath as he bowed his head in grief. Before he could begin to wallow too deeply in sorrow at the loss of his twin brother, Greggor stepped back outside.

Exiting the front door, he walked past Tomek and was humming a tune Tomek was unfamiliar with. His axes missing from his back, the large man carried a jug of lighter fluid and what appeared to be the world's largest box of matches. Organizing the cut pieces of cordwood into what resembled a Lincoln-log-style house, Tomek scoffed at the amount of lighter fluid Greggor doused the stack of wood with.

"I guess you were never a boy scout?"

"Nah, but I do know a thing or two about tying knots," Greggor replied, motioning to Tomek's waist. "But you already knew about that firsthand, huh?"

Time dragged on as Tomek stood there, tied up and watching Greggor's inner pyromaniac build the fire into a raging inferno. Wiggling back and forth, Tomek felt his restraints tighten with each flinch, and he agreed with Greggor's boasts regarding his ability to tie solid knots.

"Please stop humming."

Tomek's request was answered with more humming, this time at a much louder volume. Greggor interrupted his song.

"It's going to be dark soon, and the others are going to have plenty of questions for you. I'd suggest you save the talking for them."

"I ain't going to tell you or them shit," Tomek replied.

Greggor smiled as he pulled a red-hot, glowing piece of metal from the coals. He held it up in the air, blowing off a few clinging pieces of white coal dust before using an off-putting and poorly impersonated German accent to say, "Vee haff vays of making hyu tok."

Tomek was sure he had heard the reference before, but he was unaware the level of pure unoriginality the threat held. Still, he knew damn well what Greggor was implying.

"You can torture me all you want," Tomek replied.

Greggor stood up and waved the still glowing rod to the boy's face. Tomek could feel the heat emanating from it as he closed his eyes in preparation for the burn. After a few tense moments, Tomek had yet to feel pain but could smell seared hair as Greggor got it closer to his head on the last swipe.

"Just get on with it," Tomek yelled. "Do you even expect me to talk?"

Greggor placed the rod back in the fire, grabbing another one, fresh from the blazing bed of coals and said, "No, son, I don't expect you to talk. I expect you to die."

"I ain't your fucking son."

Tomek's raised voice reverted into full-out screams of terror as the sound of his voice joined the audible fizz of bubbling and scorching skin along his cheekbone. Greggor had laid the smoldering rod against Tomek's face, where he held it solid on the right side while he continued humming a song without a care to the world.

Pulling the rod off of Tomek's face as it began to cool, the boy's dark skin stuck to the metal piece of rebar, and Greggor was forced to tug it away, ripping off as much skin from Tomek's face as he had scorched.

"Ah, the beauty of the brand. No bleeding," Greggor said, placing the skin-covered rod back into the burning tower of heat. "I will admit that you are taking it more like a man than the last bloke did, son."

Furiously fighting through the pain in his face, Tomek fought off his body's desire to black out in shock as he concentrated on his breathing.

"I have something I must admit as well."

Greggor seemed delightfully interested. "Oh, yea? What might that be?"

"The last two guys who called me 'son' are both dead. You are about to join them." Tomek raised his badly wounded head up, looking Greggor in the eyes, and added, "Daddy."

Greggor reached down into the fire pit and selected another glowing, red rod, which he flung upwards in the air, pantomiming a man in a fencing match taking the en garde position. Greggor danced back and forth like Chi-Chi Rodriguez was famous for after making a putt and thrusted the molten-hot, makeshift sword to each side of Tomek's face, burning the tips of his ears as it passed by.

Tomek again looked up as he struggled to wiggle and dodge his head away from each, glancing thrust as much as he could. As Greggor stopped to switch out his rod for a hotter one, Tomek asked him, "What is your name?"

"Greggor, my son," he replied, openly trying to annoy Tomek with the 'son' comments mentally as he had done physically with the burns.

"Well, Mr. Greggor, I have two things I think you should know," Tomek replied.

Greggor laughed. "Okay, then. Get on with them."

"First of all, I am not your fucking son," Tomek said, making Greggor laugh even more.

"Yea, you mentioned that already."

"Secondly, you are about to die."

"Oh, really? Well, I'm not sure you are quite in the position to kill me right now," Greggor reminded him.

Tomek shrugged his shoulders enough that it could be seen underneath the rope and began to laugh.

"True, I'm not going to kill you. But he is."

Greggor whipped his head around just in time to see the blade of his own axe flash against the fire's light as it sliced through his vest, dropping gear and weapons from the front pockets while it buried itself deep into the center of his chest. The amount of pride Greggor had put into the quality razor-edge of his weapon had ensured a quick death as the blade passed through his clavicle with ease on its path inward, destroying the heart and left lung.

The large man dropped to his knees with the weapon firmly lodged in his body. With his last gasp of bloody air that bubbled with the froth of his collapsed lung, Greggor's massive body slumped into the fire he had previously built, toppling over the pyramid of logs on top of him. Greggor's legs kicked around as the coals melted the skin from his face, exposing a black and charred skull in a matter of seconds. No screams or cries were heard coming from the fire, only the smell. The smell of burning hair and flesh was present.

Tomek shook his head away from watching Greggor burn and felt a massive sense of relief as he looked into the face of the person who had just killed his abductor. A face he was sure he would never see again. A face that he now knew was not only ready to kill, but ready to do so in order to protect the island. At this moment, Tomek knew Archer was on his side. The man had now killed both Sven and Greggor and if he let Tomek live, Tomek knew Grayson Archer would be a more than useful ally here on Ascension.

Archer walked up to Tomek and began cutting at the thick ropes securing him to the tree, but with the axe now with Greggor in the improvised crematory, he was forced to use a small pocket knife, which made it a daunting job.

"I don't know who the fuck they think they are, but they all need to die."

"Agreed," said Tomek.

Archer continued freeing Tomek. "Seen you and what looked like your brother take that fall. Sorry for your loss."

"Is he dead?" Tomek asked.

"It was too foggy down there, but it didn't look good. And he didn't climb back up like you did," Archer explained. "I was following this deer or antelope or impala thing. Not sure the difference, to tell ya the truth. Anyway, the damn thing looked like it had been tore up pretty bad by something. No idea what—"

Tomek interrupted him. "I bet ya I know what. All kinds of killer shit up there. We took out a lion, saw a bear, and there are hyenas, too. You see any of them yet?"

"No, but I heard them all right."

"Nasty, fucking dogs. Hurry up. Let's get out of here," Tomek said, trying to motivate Archer into cutting faster.

"So, yea, I was right behind it, figuring it would be an easy meal, and then I came through that swampy area just as Extra Crispy over here cut the ropes and you fell. Followed you guys back to camp, and—well, in two more cuts I will have you free. Then we kill them all."

Tomek liked the new friend instantly. Having seen him take out two of the island invaders already without emotions involved, he knew that while technically, Archer was an invader as well, Tomek felt like he deserved a free pass, especially after cutting him loose.

Upon being totally loose, Tomek stretched his body out, and for the first time, the ascending pain in his face took full effect on his nervous system. The burn ached and throbbed, felling hotter than it did when he first received it. Observing he was in pain, Archer placed his hand on Tomek's shoulder to comfort him.

"We have a few hours until it is completely dark. We need to hide and take them out one by one as they come back to camp. Only three of them are left, and there are two of us."

Tomek agreed as he bent down, rifling through the supplies that Greggor had dropped from his vest. Most of them had joined him in the fire, but at this point, anything they could scrounge up would help. Placing the contents in his cargo pockets, Tomek was unsure of what exactly he would use it all for, but he was certainly glad to have it.

"Tomek," he said, introducing himself and placing his hand out for a formal greeting type of handshake. The gesture still felt foreign to him, but Old Man Hawkins had insisted that the boys learn it, a sign that meant they were becoming proper men.

"Grayson, but everyone calls me Archer," he responded, joining Tomek with his own, outstretched hand. Squeezing harder than Tomek had expected, Archer looked past him, lowered his voice, and asked inquisitively, "Tony?"

Tomek thought the man must have misheard him. "No, not Tony. The name's Tomek—"

Two, loud pops rang out from behind them, and Tomek watched in horror as Archer's face imploded on the impact of the projectiles. It was as if someone had place explosives under the man's skin, and the detonation's red, misty splatter covered Tomek as Archer's body fluttered backwards. The exit wounds on the back of his head were the size of a fist, and Tomek's new friend—his savior, his ally—was dead before his body hit the ground.

Not hesitating to see where the shots came from, Tomek took off running towards the cabin. Having no idea what he would do once getting there, it was his only near option. Two more shots rang through the air, missing him but coming close enough for him to hear the whirling and whizzing sound of the subsonic round as it passed by him and ripped the air apart in its deadly, misguided travel.

Uncle had explained to them many times about this sound. He often described it as a buzzing yellow jacket on cocaine who is all sorts of pissed off and coming to defend the hive. Tomek had no idea how in the world his mind could be thinking all of this as he was running for his life. Tomek figured that having faced his death multiple times since Uncle took his own life made him immune to the adrenaline dump that accompanied the normal fight-or-flight complex. Things slowed down, and Tomek's mind was clear in these situations. Tomek felt a smile come across his face as the third round hit a log behind him. It did sound like the yellow jacket Uncle had described, only higher pitched than he imagined.

Reaching the corner of the cabin, Tomek skirted around the edge as he bent over and attempted to catch his breath. With the building between him and the shooter, he dug through his pants' cargo pockets that where full of the items he pulled off Greggor and located a small, switchblade knife. It was more of the roadside gas station, impulse-buy variety, but it was deadly sharp, like the previous owner's axe, and would have to work for now.

Peeking his head around the corner, he saw the shooter up against the opposite wall of the house, walking cautiously and hugging the wall tight. Tomek knew he had the better position and waited for his opponent to break the invisible, ninety-degree, northwest corner of the house. Kneeling down, he planned on thrusting the knife through the bottom of the jaw, instantly taking out the subject and hopefully doing so without another shot being fired.

Tomek's heartrate had returned to normal as he watched the barrel of the pistol break the plane. Tomek knew this was the moment and that his exact location was unknown to his opponent. With an aggressive, vertical pounce, Tomek went to thrust the knife into the gunman's throat. Just as he reached the apex of his attacking move, his body went completely limp.

Tomek hit the ground, feeling the pain of his branded face slamming into and being dragged down the wooden siding of the house on his descent. He blinked twice; trying to focus his eyes, but was unsuccessful. He then realized his eyes were not deceiving him, and he really was looking at four boots as everything went dark.

18 STARS

The stars illuminated the dark sky in breathtaking abundance as he came to. Opening his heavy eyelids and struggling to make sense of the new position he found himself in, the pain set in, wrathfully confronting his body like a pissed off tidal wave of hate. The unsettling lack of feeling in his legs was only second to the drastic numbness of his right arm from the elbow down. Looking down at his legs, a burst of adrenalin allowed him to kick them wildly into the air. The adrenalin was thanks to him seeing the lack of anything solid below him.

Rubbing the crusted and dried blood away from his eyes that had built up while he remained unconscious, Drake only then realized he was tangled up in the bridge's already suspect rope system. While the pain was intense, it reminded him that he was, in fact, still alive.

Dangling there above the jagged rocks and unforgiving waters, Drake felt helpless as he swayed in the gentle breeze and surveyed his situation. He quickly realized that if not for the bow strapped to his pack getting snagged, his view of the stars would be from heaven, not earth.

"Heaven," he murmured to himself, laughing at the notion of his being accepted past the pearly gates with the amount of blood he had on his hands. Drake understood the whole "ask for forgiveness" aspect of Old Man Hawkins' religion, but he figured that didn't apply to him at this point.

With blood flow returning to his arm as he moved it around and massaged life back into his veins, he suspected the prolonged suspension had the same effect on his legs, which suffered the same, tingling loss of sensation. While he couldn't feel his legs, they still hurt. It was an odd sensation, and one he hoped wouldn't last as he began to untangle his pack and climb.

Pulling hand over hand and struggling up the combination rope-and-plank vertical ladder, Drake's strong arms made up for the weakness in his legs, and upon cresting the top, he laid flat on his stomach and exhaled hard, his breath vaporizing into the chill of the night's air.

Drake's already brief rest was cut short at the sound of something larger than a human clumsily meandering through the swamp to his left. Darkness had set in prior to his awakening, and Drake had been unable to look for Tomek below the bridge. The presence of the unknown beast kept him from yelling Tomek's name in an attempt to locate his twin. Although he knew that if Tomek had fallen, no amount of calling his name was going to do a damn thing. Not tonight, anyway.

With his brother's fate uncertain and the potential of a man-eater closing in on him, Drake vigorously shook his legs, willing the blood flow to return to normal so he could attempt to run. Drake stood up, using the bow as a half crutch. He knew that, even on good legs, the large, open field he needed to cross to find the safety of the round stone shed would leave plenty of opportunity for anything that wanted to dine on his flesh to do so. However, he knew that he had to try.

After struggling to cover the first fifty yards, the feeling had mostly returned to his extremities, and he stopped to shake the lactic acid out and catch his breath. The unknown cause of the sound in the swamp was still present, but Drake was glad to see that he had put a decent chunk of distance between himself and the edge. Turning backwards, he walked at a quickening pace, keeping an eye on the spot where he expected the predator to emerge from.

Reaching down to his side, Drake pressed the dangling, worn, leather quiver against his body to keep it from swinging and making noise as it hit the side of his leg. It was then he realized the quiver had been crushed and was practically empty. Every arrow shaft except one had fallen out during his tumble down the bridge. Drake removed the one remaining arrow, and prior to nocking it, realized the broadhead had snapped off and was gone as well. He knew one, wood-tipped arrow shaft would be useless on anything bigger than a rabbit. There was a lot he did not know about the island, but he was sure that there was not an abundance of man-eating rabbits present, making anything else in the swamp that might possibly eat meat trouble for him at this point.

An involuntary bead of sweat began to break on his forehead as he scrambled back the way he'd come. Being armed with only a dull knife on his hip in the daylight was less than desirable. In the dark, he knew that making it to the shelter was his only choice. Drake's legs jumped back into life as he slung his bow back over his shoulder and began the sprint.

Looking back only once as he ran, he was surprised at what he saw exiting from the edge of the swampland. It was not a bear, lion, or even hyenas. He saw a flickering light. The flickering light of Ricardo Stratton's tiny, Bic lighter partially illuminated the wetland game trail he was using to make it through the swamp. Unwilling to stop in order to appease his curiosity, he knew that if the source of the light was by chance Tomek, his brother knew the location of the shelter and would for sure be headed his way.

The metal door flung open easier than Drake had expected it to as he slipped inside the round rock structure. Drake wrapped his hands around the hinges, hoping their creaking would not alert the entire island of his whereabouts. It was only then he looked back and again saw Ricardo with his flickering light. The combination of the almost perfectly full moon against the massive, calm, lake waters provided enough light for Drake to instantly realize that it was not his brother who had exited the swamp.

Unable to see details of the subject who was now at the edge of the bridge Drake had just climbed from, Drake secured the door and readied his knife. The thought crossed his mind that, with the mix of malfunctioning legs and his desire to reach the shelter, Drake had not paid any attention to trying to hide his own tracks. He was safe in the shed again for now, but he hoped that the tall man with the flickering light lacked even the slightest tracking skills. However, Drake knew that Ricardo most likely didn't know of his existence, and there was a good chance that the hyenas might eliminate the threat he represented as well.

Minutes passed, although they seemed like hours. All remained silent, and after a few hours, Drake felt confident that Ricardo had moved on elsewhere. Drake stretched his legs and bumped around in the dark room. His only source of light was the small moonbeams that penetrated between the gaps of the round rocks.

Feeling his quiver, he was reminded of the lone arrow shaft he had remaining. Drake removed it and opened up his folding knife. After two or three shaving passes, he could tell that without the proper light, sharpening the shaft to a point would be a futile experience. Drake could feel with each pass as the sharp knife dug too deep and removed more wood than he wanted.

Looking around the room, he found it oddly humorous that Tomek and he had not checked any of the drawers under the shed's workbench area after last night's hyena attack. Being awakened by the helicopter's arrival meant they rushed out. Drake fumbled around, opening drawer after drawer in the hopes of finding some kind of weapon, but the contents were limited to a few tools, dining utensils, and some random fishing gear.

Opening the last drawer, Drake was delighted to find a twelve-pack of chemical light sticks, or as Uncle called them, chem lights. Drake ripped the first one out of its package and bent the pliable, plastic housing until hearing the familiar pop of the interior floating cylinder. The green luminescence of the light was instant and bright. The small room was now flooded with the bright, neon-green light.

Uncle had always picked up the smaller, civilian glow stick lights on his trips into town, and the boys knew he must have gotten them from The Hawk's Nest, because it was an item they often stocked overnight while working in the store.

Drake fondly thought about that first Halloween they spent in Pine Run and how the kids all adorned the lights as necklaces and various parts of their silly garb. Tomek and he acted like they found the entire thing pointless, but both secretly liked the idea of dressing up to hide their identity in plain sight. Plus, there was candy, which was the rarest of all rare treats in their woodland life with Uncle.

Now, he stood basking in the glow of a chem light in a shack, alone on an island in the middle of Lake Michigan, and found himself feeling nostalgic and alone. He was thankful for the chem light. It brought a sense of comfort to his situation, but his circumstances could not be any different now than the last time he relied on them for light.

The light also provided Drake with a boost of motivation to go through the contents of the drawers again, on the chance that he may have missed something useful while previously doing so in the dark. Sadly at first, the remnants of a once-useful toolshed provided him with nothing more than some duct tape and screwdrivers he placed in his pack for no other reason than possibly using them as stabbing weapons.

The leftover kitchen utensils included plates, bowls, and a few random assortments of forks and spoons.

Not even a butter knife? Drake thought to himself.

His despair faded upon opening the second drawer from the bottom, again looking over the multiple, old hand tools, when he saw the mill bastard file. The file opened a whole new world of opportunity to him. Not only could he sharpen the screwdrivers' flat heads into useful, puncture-sharp weapons, he now had everything he needed to improvise a broadhead.

With a few knives and at least one good arrow, Drake was confident he could reach the cabin, where he knew the rest of his supplies would be.

At least, they were there yesterday, he thought to himself, remembering that the helicopter had headed that way after the death of Sven.

Opening the utensil drawer, Drake selected what appeared to be an ordinary spoon. Being that the contents of the drawer were wet from a leaking roof and there was not a speck of oxidization on the spoon, Drake knew it was made of stainless steel. While he had never made broadheads from stainless steel spoons before, he had made them from just about every other material, including rocks and the leg bones of deer. This process, he figured, would be no different.

Without a heat source present, Drake struggled to flatten out the concave bowl of the spoon head. He was thankful that a hammer was included in the leftover tool kit but knew he could have done the same with the right size rock and a little more time. As happy as he was to have the hammer, he was glad upon being done with it. He knew the sound of the impact on the metal would let anyone in the general area know he was inside the shed. Drake only hoped that the sound of the waves lapping around the shores below and the interior walls of the shelter were enough to hide the sound. But with each strike, his ears throbbed with pain a little more as the sounds reverberated inside the small, enclosed area.

Using the file, Drake started at the back edge of the blade and slowly stroked forward. Knowing Uncle always preferred his edge blades at a precise, twenty-two-and-a-half degree angle, Drake tried his best to make each stroke replicate the next. Feeling the burr starting to form, Drake spun the spoon around and repeated the process for the opposite edge. Within a few minutes, Drake had a respectable edge on both sides of the spoon head. He knew that it was not up Uncle's standards, but he was proud of his ingenuity either way.

Dragging his thumb across the edge he knew it was sharp enough to kill just about anything. Drake reached down to remove the arrow shaft from his quiver and quickly remembered that the quiver itself was crafted from old, worn leather. Uncle would often claim that old leather just happened to be "the perfect material for stropping a blade in any situation." Drake did not fully agree with Uncle on this, as he liked the simplicity of using his denim pants to strop a knife on his thigh. The cotton, military surplus, cargo pants he currently wore would not do the trick, so Drake reverted to Uncle's time-tested technique.

Laying the quiver down and pressing it flat against the maple workbench, Drake spat on the flat leather and rubbed in the moisture to liven the hide up just a bit. Stropping the blades back and forth across the worn leather of the old quiver, he caught himself counting down the strokes out loud, just as Uncle did with each pass. Building a rhythm with the sound of the blade edge's stropping across the leather, it was almost musical in syncopation and chant.

1, 2, 3, on this side.

1, 2, 3 on that side.

1, 2, on this side.

1, 2, on that side.

1, on this side.

1, on that side.

"If you're never sure about your life, always be sure you have a sharp knife."

Drake ended the songful, stropping sequence the same as he always remembered Uncle doing so.

Lifting the flattened, and now deadly sharp, spoon head up against the green glow of his chem light, Drake marveled at what he had done. Holding the head in one hand and the spoon handle in the other, Drake worked them up and down vigorously and felt the metal grow hot at the fulcrum of the bend he was creating. Keeping at this for a few more seconds weakened the spoon enough to make it snap, and it left him with a detached, two-blade, Howard Hill-looking broadhead.

Uncle would be proud, he thought to himself.

Drake then turned his focus to the arrow shaft and was relieved to find that it had snapped relatively clean at the end. This gave him enough length to attach the new head to. Drake splintered the end of the arrow's wood with a single slit of his knife and wedged the spoon head into its new home. He was surprised at how well the wood held on to the head, but he knew that it would take more than this to keep it in place.

Drake laughed as his eyes focused on the roll of duct tape.

Really? He said in his head.

However, given the circumstances, the roll of silver-gold was just the thing he needed. Pulling a full-width stripe from the roll and then slicing it down into a thin strand, Drake wrapped the arrow shaft around the area where it met the razor spoon head. Drake's technique mirrored the exact thing he would do with natural sinew. The only thing he was missing was a dab of pine tar as glue, but he figured the adhesive of the duct tape would provide plenty of holding power.

Drake nocked the arrow and pulled it back to test the length and feel.

Perfect, he thought.

With his task complete for the night, Drake peered between the rocks of the wall to see the moon close to crossing the sky. He knew that the sun would be rising within a few hours and figured he should probably attempt to get at least some sleep. Lying on the ground, the glow of the light was more than his eyelids could filter out. Drake hated to waste the chem light's effectiveness, but he slid it down into the quiver to drown out its cast.

Drake quickly drifted into sleep but remained awake enough to know that tomorrow the only thing that mattered was finding Tomek. Dead or alive, they must be together.

19 CUTS

The metallic, iron taste of blood jolted Tomek as he woke up. Pain radiated throughout his head, and his sight was obstructed from a massive amount of swelling. Tomek knew that he must have taken one hell of a beating and was at least thankful that it happened while he was unconscious.

His hands again were bound behind his back with a zip tie-type of handcuff as he looked at the fire pit. A thick rope had been wrapped around his chest, securing him to a wooden chair. The rope was very tight and did an excellent job of preventing him from fully expanding his lungs for a deep breath. Short, pulsating puffs of air were all Tomek could muster in order to keep his body oxygenated.

Greggor's body had been removed, and he found it odd that a man would cook his meal over a bed of coals that had contained human remains; but that is just what Garran was in the process of doing. Tomek didn't want to admit it to himself, but he did think the hotdog roasting in front of him smelled absolutely enchanting.

"Good evening, sunshine," Garran said as he slid the dog off of the skewer and into a bun.

Tomek didn't answer him.

"Wanna bite?" Garran asked as he bit into the meat, laughing.

"No, thanks. Already had a barbecue earlier tonight with your buddy. You know, the one who was well done?" Tomek said, referencing the missing, charred body of Greggor.

Tomek regretted his response the minute Garran's knife slammed down into the top of his foot, pinning it to the ground beneath him. Tomek kicked and squirmed at the protruding handle, dislodging the blade while rolling around in pain.

Garran sighed. "I don't know who the hell you are, or how the hell you got yourself on my island, but I can assure you this, you will soon be talking to me with respect."

Tomek decided to break his silence in an attempt to show his newest captor that he knew some information about him. It was a bluff, but he had heard Archer say the name.

"Fuck you, Tony."

Garran enjoyed another mouthful of his frank and smirked. "Nice try. Tony is my boy, and that pussy is in the cabin right now, thinking about why he couldn't take the shot. He had the perfect opportunity to kill that Archer fuck, but no. Tony—my own, goddamned son—didn't have the balls, the intestinal fortitude, to pull the goddamned trigger. So, no, you little, black spook fuck, I am not Tony. The name is Garran, in case you actually give a shit."

"Nice to meet ya," Tomek said, spitting out blood and a piece of broken tooth onto the ground.

"It is nice to see that after I beat the hell out of you and stab your foot that you still have a sense of humor."

"I am going to kill you, just like I killed that axe-toting, ass-fuck friend of yours," Tomek said, taking credit for Archer's removal of Greggor. He knew that Garran wouldn't know or need to know the truth.

"Now you are straight up telling jokes," Garran replied. "I love it."

Tomek felt himself becoming dizzy and drifted in and out consciousness. The next time he awoke, he was now sitting in what he thought was some kind of metal chair. His hands were still bound but now laid in his lap. A belt was strung across his thighs and around the bottom of the seat. That, combined with the rope used to originally secure him to the tree now being around his chest, meant he was again fully imprisoned.

"Welcome back," Garran said, "I have some questions for you."

Tomek doubted that he had any of the answers that Garran would be looking for and knew that he would most likely refuse to give him any information. After all, what could he do to Tomek that could be worse than what Greggor had already done with his branding of his face?

"First things first, how did you get on my fucking island?"

"I swam," Tomek said as he shrugged his shoulders.

Garran's fist slammed into Tomek's chest, impacting his ribs.

"To be honest, your face is a little fucked up. Time to hurt the rest of your body," Garran said, explaining his new line of punishment for Tomek. "Let's try this one: Where is Ricardo?"

"If he was up your ass, you would know where he was."

Tomek's defiant answer earned him another blow to his opposite ribcage, and he tumbled to the side, unable to breathe. Rolling around in the chair, Tomek gasped at air and eventually was able to quench his lungs' desire for life.

"I don't know who you are, or who Ricardo or Tony is either. I haven't seen anybody on this island until you arrived in your fucking chopper."

Tomek saw no reason to shed light on the existence of Drake, being that he had no clue if he was alive or not and the only other person he somewhat trusted on the island, Archer, was dead.

Garran lowered his brow, looking at him with a mouthful of hotdog. "So, you're just out here all alone and mysteriously swam up to my island, huh?"

"I am a good swimmer," Tomek replied.

Garran again smirked and seemed to enjoy the little bit of humor that Tomek had left in him. "Well, then, you must be awful lonely."

"There is a difference between being lonely and being alone," said Tomek.

"Clever. Who taught you that? Your daddy?"

"No, my Uncle."

Garran stood up to stoke the fire, adding another log to it. "So, this uncle of yours, did he bring you here to poach my animals?"

"No," Tomek replied, looking down. "He is dead. He is a ghost."

Upon hearing the word 'ghost,' Garran froze in his tracks, and even Tomek could see through his swollen eye that the comment had resonated with the man.

Tom H. had become the man that the island's murderous hunters now referred to as "The ghost." The name had been unfamiliar to Tony, but the twins knew Tom H. all too well. Tom H. was not known to Drake and Tomek as "The ghost" but as "Uncle."

"So, you know of The Ghost?" Garran asked, breaking his silence.

"I know a lot of things," Tomek replied.

Garran sat back down in his camp chair, across the fire from Tomek, and searched his mind deeply in regards to exactly who Tomek could possibly be and if he really did know the island's ghost. Garran pulled a knife from a scabbard on his belt; Tomek recognized it as the same one he had taken off of Greggor after he met his demise in the fire.

Garran placed the needle-like tip of the blade on the top of Tomek's sternum, pressing it against the indent at the top of brachial tube. The knife's pressure alone, without cutting, caused pain, and it intensified as Garran sadistically began thinly slicing upwards, cutting across Tomek's throat, and stopping at the chin. He then wiped the blade clean of blood on Tomek's shoulder.

"I know that you have some knowledge about the things I am asking. And I know you think you have knowledge that might keep you alive. Well,

I would have to remind you that the greatest enemy of knowledge is not ignorance. No, not at all. The greatest enemy of knowledge is the illusion of knowledge."

Tomek began to shake nervously as the blade was slicing. The thought of choking on his own blood had caused him to momentarily lose his composure. He found it a great relief when Garran stopped at his chin and that the cut was purely superficial. Garran could have easily slashed his throat, but for some reason, he did not.

"So, I'll ask you one more time. Where is Ricardo?"

Tomek looked him defiantly in the eyes and replied, "Just kill me."

"You see, life is strange, and as you watched earlier with our dear departed dipshit Archer, I have no problem with ending a life. Just to be clear, I don't want to die. My son does not want to die, and my friends don't want to die. It is just a damn shame that you are in such a hurry to."

"Were you not listening?" Tomek asked. "I said just fucking kill me."

Tomek was almost pleading at this point, pushing Garran to see how far he could get the man to go.

"I don't know much about you, but I bet if you had a crystal ball and could see the future, you didn't see yourself dying like this, like a little bitch asking to be put down," Garran replied as he pulled his side arm out, racking a shell from the magazine into the chamber.

Tomek looked at him with disgust, ready to die, and said, "Everyone wants to know their future, until they do."

Garran pulled the hammer back and placed the gun against Tomek's forehead. Impressed, he said, "I'll have to admit it, son, those are some epic last words."

The tiny sound of the hammer hitting the brass percussion cap of the primer reverberated like a slow-motion carnival in Tomek's ears. He had not expected to hear the percussion blast of the pistol as the round exited the barrel as clearly as he did from such a close range. His eyes were clenched tighter than they ever had been, and he felt that at least now he could be with Uncle.

Tomek was glad that at the moment of the gun's discharge he felt zero pain. There was no bright light; there were no pearly gates, no flames, no eternal damnation, no demons, or even angels. Tomek opened his eyes, and the only light he saw was that of the same, cracking campfire.

Is this heaven? He wondered.

If it was, in this version of heaven, there was only one angel, and that angel was named Tony. Tomek looked across the fire to see a boy his own age standing there, shaking in pure shock. Tony had just killed Garran, his own father, who now lay motionless at Tomek's feet.

20 RATTLE

The sound of the distant gunshots earlier in the night, coming from the cabin side of the island, had been muffled by the wind and waves of the island. However, the pistol shot that took Garran's life at daybreak echoed across the island like a symphony of death carried upon the wind.

Drake awoke. Stretching his legs, he was surprised at how refreshed he actually felt. Being that a helicopter and now a gunshot served as his morning alarm clocks the last two days, the fact that he had two nights in a row with decent sleep was appreciated.

"Time to find Tomek," he thought to himself as he unlatched the shed's metal door and stepped out of the bunker. The sun illuminated the east side of the cliffs as it broke from the horizon. Watching the sun erupt over the crest of the bowl from the cabin area below was definitely impressive, but as Drake watched the sun rise first over the lake edge and then the island edge, he knew that the previous sunrises he had encountered failed in comparison to this one.

Drake thought back to the map of the island they had found in the book of names. Checking his backpack, he was disappointed that it was missing. He knew that if Tomek was not dead in the now bridgeless gorge that he would be on the opposite side. Drake figured Tomek would have looked for him and then headed back to camp to avenge his death.   Peering   over the edge of the inlet, Drake was not only relieved but also motivated by the lack of a body in the rocks below the fallen bridge. With a clear-sky morning and zero fog, Drake searched the bottom with his eyes from the ledge, confirming that just like him, somehow, Tomek had not fallen to his death.

The only question now was if Tomek wasn't dead, where was he?

The beautiful, chilly air of the morning fogged as it left Drake's lungs. He turned north and planned to work his way around the edge and across the meadow, where he would have the best opportunity to see any approaching danger. This also gave him the best chance to pick up a track on the sandy dirt path that wove through the area back to the wall.

As the first hour of Drake's hike passed, hunger set in. Taking off his backpack, Drake rummaged through it and sat down with his back against an old hickory tree. The tree and its shaggy bark seemed out of place in the island's meadow to Drake, but then again, everything was weird on this island.

Why would the trees be any different?

Other than having no water and choking down the dryness of the MRE, it went down smoothly and provided him the nourishment needed to complete the two-hour hike he had left until reaching his destination at the wall. Inventorying the contents that remained in his pack, he saw an orange flare gun and a few other things he had forgotten he grabbed from the cabin, like a pen and some rubber bands. However, when it came to the flare gun, Uncle certainly had never used anything of the sort, and the signaling device was foreign to him. Other than a brief, how-to session with Annette when she gave it to them, he had yet to mess with it at all.

Drake unfastened the break-open chamber design and ensured that it was loaded and ready to go, just in case his sister's plane was to fly over unexpectedly. He would not be able to raise the flag in time to signal her, but he knew the flare would be just as effective. Cocking the hammer back and then releasing it into the safety position, he felt like it was a pretty straightforward tool. Enjoying the sun, as it had now burnt off the shadows of the island, Drake sat there cocking and uncocking the flare gun as he finished off the last of his dehydrated pineapple chunks. He always saved them for last, treating them like a dessert.

A gentle, westerly breeze changed his brief, carefree demeanor quickly. He couldn't hear the bear, but he could smell him. The scent was the same, rotgut musk that saturated the wind when he and Tomek had found the same grizzly feeding on the doe that Tomek had run an arrow through. Drake knew that if he was able to smell the bear, he must be close. He also was well aware that the bear's nose would be working to its full extent in return.

Drake jumped up, keeping his back to the tree and his eyes on the waving, meadow grass. Picking up his pack, he placed the flare in his backpack and slung it back over his shoulders. He was downwind of the bear and knew that chances were good that the bear had not smelled him or his food. Drake removed the razor spoon-tipped arrow he had made only hours ago from the quiver and nocked it on the string.

Moving slowly along the path that edged up to the rock-lined cliff, Drake labored to make each step silent. His eyes were drawn into the grasses ahead of him, where he figured the brown, giant bruin would appear.

Having moved almost three hundred yards along the meadow path, the smell was just as strong as it had been originally back at his lunch spot against the hickory tree. With no sign of the bear yet, Drake knew that it must have been moving parallel to him but staying just out of visual range. Glancing up the path, he knew that the pinch point where Tomek's lion had taken the leap of faith was just ahead, and if the bear showed himself near that group of trees, Drake worried he would be trapped.

With the tangle of trees in view, Tomek moved towards them cautiously, with his bow at the ready. He had his doubts in regards to the arrow's usefulness on a brown bear, but it was all he had other than the knife on his hip. Moving closer, step by silent step, Drake finally locked eyes on what he believed to now be Ascension Island's top predator, the grizzly bear.

The massive animal had found the only shady spot in the meadow, in the clump of cliffside trees, and was apparently enjoying a midafternoon siesta. Drake still had the wind in his favor and crept closer to the sleeping hulk. Taking in the totality of his situation, he found himself in quite the predicament. Continuing along the silent path toward the wall and cabin meant crossing within ten feet of the beast. His only other option would be to enter the meadow and walk through the thick, waist-high grass.

Option number two would keep him the furthest distance from the bear, but at the same time, opened him up to a multitude of other dangers. Once in the taller grasses, he knew that he would have to crawl to stay out of sight. Also, this would force him to move upwind of the bear, and the wafting stink of human scent would surely raise the brute from his slumber. The last two concerns were the largest for Drake. Once in the grass, his vision would be severely limited. This would make him an extremely easy target for any lion or hyena that fancied a midday snack.

"Let sleeping bears lie," he heard Uncle's voice say.

Drake thought back to all the times he had heard Uncle use the phrase and could not remember a single incident where their discussion involved an actual bear. Uncle most often said it when referencing Tomek and his temper, urging Drake not to pick on him or rile him up on certain topics. In those cases, Tomek was the bear, which was much different than what he faced now. Still though, the saying held true, and Drake agreed with Uncle as he headed off of the beaten path, sliding his way into the blinding brush land of the island's meadow.

Drake quickly found that, even upwind of the snoring bruin, he could detect the pungent odor of its musky smell. Drake quivered the arrow and slung the bow over his shoulder prior to dropping to his hands and knees. Crawling at a snail's pace, he worked his way back and forth over the grassy ground and popped his head up every ten feet to check on the status of the bear. Having made it almost past the clump of trees without arousing suspicion, he picked up the pace, thinking he was just about in the clear.

Lifting his head up one last time, it was not what he saw that caused his heart to jump nearly to top of his throat, it was what he heard. The rattling tail of an eastern massasauga rattlesnake jolted every nerve in his body. Michigan only has one venomous snake, and Drake knew that it was a deadly bite he was not willing to chance. Combined with the fact that this island held the vast amount of species that it did, he would not be surprised if other species of deadlier snakes had been imported as well.

The imposing, vibrating buzz of the snake's tail end was not only loud and intimidating, it was also invisible. Darting his eyes in every direction, he could not see the snake, only hear it, but he knew it was close, too close. Frozen in a position between a kneel and a crawl, his leg muscles began to ache as he watched the bear sleeping twenty yards away and listened to the death rattle of the fanged viper only feet away.

Drake pulled his back leg up to his chest and stood up. His movement was met with another rattle alarm being set off. Now, it was clear that he had violated the personal space of two rattlesnakes. Both of which, thanks to Mother Nature's exceptional job of camouflaging, he could not see. For all he knew, he was standing on one that would sink its hypodermic needle-like fangs into him as soon as he moved. Drake knew that waiting out the snakes would be an exercise in futility, and the bear would be awake before long, forcing his hand anyway.

Drake decided that death by bear would be advantageous, based on his hope that a mauling would kill him much quicker than that of the venom. With three bounds, he again was on the cleared path, now a mere twelve feet from the clump of trees that served as the grizzly's bedroom.

The smell at this distance was almost unbearable, and even though Drake was in the clear to head south, away from the danger of the bear, he couldn't help but take one last, long look at it. While staring at the immense head of the animal and noticing the massive amount of flies that covered the entire hide, he realized for the first time the smell was not the odor of bear. It was the odor of death.

Closing the distance and now standing directly at the foot of the bear, he confirmed that it was not sleeping at all. The blondish-brown, ripped-open fur along the belly of the animal made it clearly evident that someone had somehow been close enough to the animal to eviscerate it there on that exact spot. Drake grabbed the front paw and dragged it over the top of its head. Using a good amount of strength, he rolled the bear on its back and saw the rotting intestines and stomach on the ground under the animal.

Drake brushed away a small amount of flies that had found their meal ticket on the carcass. He knew that the kill was relatively fresh based on the condition of the stomach lining and the amount of blood that was still wet on the ground. The slice along the belly and a puncture wound near the back of the jaw were the only two wounds Drake could see on the animal. Drake rubbed his hand through the thick burr-like fur on the skull between the ears.

Not expecting an answer from the bear, of course, he still asked, "What the hell cut you open like this in a fight?"

"I did," Ricardo answered as he dropped down from his hiding perch in the tree behind Tomek.

Drake recognized him as one of the men from the helicopter and figured he must have been the source of the flickering light the night before.

"You must be good with them knives," Drake said, backing away while commenting on the obscene amount of cutlery Ricardo had attached to his body.

"The best," the butcher Ricardo replied.

Drake and Ricardo circled each other as if they were in a high school wrestling match or perhaps even an Olympic fencing duel. However, only Ricardo held a lance in the form of a machete-type blade featuring a custom-made handguard that resembled a set of spiked, brass knuckles.

Drake removed the bow from his shoulders and reached his hand down towards the single arrow in his quiver.

"Ah, ah, ah," Ricardo said, waving his finger back and forth, scolding Drake like a child who had done something against his parent's will.

Drake moved his arm away from the quiver and set it on the ground, along with the bow. His pack was then added to the pile. The standoff continued as Drake unsheathed the small, four-inch-blade knife on his hip and held it up tactically with the cutting edge facing down.

"That is more like it," Ricardo said with a smile.

"So, how do you see this working out?" Drake asked causally.

"I am going to cut you open, spill your guts like I did Baloo over there," Ricardo replied, referencing *The Jungle Book*.

The irony of him saying that was not lost on Drake as he recalled the Sheriff who had named both him and Tomek *Mowgli*.

"Going to cut me open, huh?"

"Yup," Ricardo said, quickly stepping closer towards Drake, which made him spring back reactively.

"Cut me open just like that helicopter blade did to your buddy, huh?" Drake said.

"Not my buddy. My brother," Ricardo yelled as he ran forward, slashing the machete through the air.

Drake ducked the first brush and felt the wind of the blade's errant swing break upon his neck. Ricardo backhand swung the blade in a return attempt to maim Drake, but again, the twin was sly enough to avoid contact.

Drake moved on the offensive, trying to bury his blade into the neck of his opponent, but his strike was too long. Without the proper reach, the blade missed its intended target as well. This brought Drake closer than he wanted to Ricardo, and the price was paid as Ricardo slammed his forehead into

Drake's, knocking him back and to the ground. Drake became dizzy from the blow that had also jarred his knife into the air, leaving him defenseless on the ground.

The Glasgow kiss was not something Drake had been taught to defend against, and he found the strategy of using one's head absolutely absurd but could not deny the effectiveness of the move. Drake had landed on top of his backpack and lay on his back, looking up as the man's blade was thrusting vertically towards his chest. Rolling to the right, he avoided the stab wound, but the blade sliced the back of his arm along the triceps as Ricardo removed it from the sand and attempted again to drive it home into the middle of Drake's body. Drake rolled to the left this time, which extended his life as the blade sliced its way into the pack.

The sound of the flare gun going off inside the bag was a surprise to both subjects, and the bag burst into a crackling ball of flames. Punching up as hard as he could in a striking motion, Drake's fist made contact with the last remaining Stratton brother's family jewels, dropping the man to his knee. Drake slid out from beneath him and picked up the bow and quiver.

Ricardo got back to his feet just as the spoon-tipped arrow entered his upper left shoulder. Drake watched as the shaft buried itself deep, but did not pass through, a circumstance he assumed was due to the makeshift cutting edge he had achieved with simple cutlery. Not happy with the shot placement as well, Drake knew his arrow was only inches away from the man's heart. He had not aimed small enough, picking a spot the way in which he had been trained by Uncle. In his haste to get the shot off, Drake had fired at center mass without concentration.

Ricardo, standing next to the fully engulfed bag, stumbled backwards, with the strap looped around his left foot. Looking down, he was able to kick the bag loose from his foot and fling it behind them into the meadow. Weakened from the protruding arrow shaft and the blood loss it resulted in,

Drake knew that, while the arrow had missed the man's heart, was as good as dead. It just would not be the instant kill, which would have been ideal.

Ricardo fell to the ground and rolled to his back. Grabbing the shaft, he snapped it off and threw it to the side. With a quickly growing grassfire raging behind them, being fed by the relentless winds of the lake, Drake walked up to Ricardo and looked at him breathing hard. From Drake's position above him, it seemed that Ricardo's eyes were fixated on the twin's boots.

"Don't move, Don't fucking move," Ricardo threatened.

From above, looking down on the situation, Drake admired the quickness of the fire that had overtaken the majority of the huge meadow as it now spread as wildfires tend to do. Drake also realized that Ricardo's demand to not move was not a demand at all. It was a plea, a plea from a dying man who would rather bleed out due to his archery wound than be bitten by the rattlesnake that remained coiled eight inches from his head, just off the toe of Drake's boot.

Drake remained silent and kicked the tail of the snake, causing the reptile to propel itself forward into a forceful strike and bury its fangs directly into Ricardo's cheek. The man screamed in agony, writhing around towards the fire and into what Drake guessed was an endless pit of fire-fleeing, venomous snakes.

Drake turned around and proceeded down the path towards the north end of the island. The fire blocked his shortest route to the wall, and he would have to walk around the entire island again to reach his destination with hopes of finding his brother. Drake was not looking forward to a trek across the unburnt sections of land he knew would be full of predators looking to escape the blaze, but he had zero other options. Unarmed, his pace matched that of a mid-race jogger, and he continued on, never looking back at the destruction of the rampant inferno behind him.

21 ALIKE

"Um, thanks, I guess," Tomek said, looking at Tony as he took in the situation, realizing what had happened.

"I didn't do it for you," Tony replied as he walked up to the body and stroked his fingers across his father's eyelids, closing them.

"That is your dad, right?" Tomek asked.

Tony nodded. "*Was* my dad."

"Well, again, thanks for saving me," Tomek mentioned again with an awkward smile.

"You are not saved. My father was a monster, and his friends are monsters, too. I am not like them; I could never be like them. Ricardo is out there somewhere. He is a monster like my dad," Tony said.

"What do you think this Ricardo fella is going to do when he finds out you killed your pops?" Tomek asked.

"He will probably want to kill me, and that is not going to happen," Tony replied nonchalantly, causing Tomek to wonder if Garran really was Tony's first kill or if his bravos was just born out of complete shock.

"Please understand that I am in no way disagreeing with you, but you do sound pretty monstrous yourself, talking like that." Tomek tried to make a point but regretted saying it the moment it left his lips.

"I am going to kill Ricardo, and then, with my dad dead, no one will ever be hunted on this island again," Tony explained.

Tomek instantly understood the motivations of the boy his own age. The hunting and killing of humans for sport was something that fell on the dark side of even Tomek's jaded moral compass.

"Cut me loose, and I will help you."

"Not going to happen. Not yet, anyway," Tony replied.

"I can help you survive. I live on this island."

"Consider yourself evicted," Tony said as he turned and walked away.

Tomek watched as Tony entered the cabin for a few moments and then walked back out with his rifle in tow. Without a word, Tony racked the bolt on the weapon and walked directly back up to the fire pit, placing the barrel of the gun on Tomek's head.

"Stay here, be quiet, and if he shows up, you tell him I am dead," Tony said.

Tomek nodded, being that he was not in much of a position to negotiate.

Turning around, Tony looked over the back of the cabin to the cliffs above the wall and under his breath exclaimed, "What the hell?"

The amber glow of Drake's grassfire was now visible from below. With the entire meadow now engulfed in a wind-fed wildfire, the smoke billowed high into the air and hung like a thick cloud over the entire island. Neither Tony nor Tomek were aware of the cause, but both were concerned for separate reasons.

Tomek hoped the fire was associated with Drake in some way or another. At this point, he was desperate to know if his brother had survived, and if he did, he knew Drake could have set the fire for a multitude of reasons.

To Tony, the fire provided yet another obstacle to ending his nightmare time on the hellish island. Tony was hell-bent on not leaving the island alive until he confirmed that Ricardo was dead. He could not risk more lies and more deaths to the sick life-and-death game of chase that his father and friends enjoyed playing.

"That has got to be one hell of a fire," Tomek said.

Tony's response came as he walked toward the imprisoned twin and said, "No shit."

Those would be the last words Tomek would hear from Tony as the butt of the rifle's stock impacted the top of Tomek's head, knocking him out completely.

Hours later, Tomek's eyes creased open, and he was again angry to still be alive and in pain. With Tony out of sight, Tomek began to think. Waiting for what seemed like an eternity, he knew in reality it was closer to ten minutes. Feeling secure that Tony was long gone, Tomek began to wiggle and squirm in an attempt to free himself from the rope and chair. Tomek's side-rocking and pushing efforts were hindered by his inability to capture a full breath of air, thanks to the extreme tightness of the rope.

Gaining momentum with each push of his legs, the chair tipped, and while being unable to break his fall, Tomek's already tortured face again received the brunt of the ground's impact. He had hoped the chair would break, allowing him out of at least the ropes, which would enable him to start working on the plastic, zip tied cuffs, but his wishes remained unfulfilled.

Now lying on the ground, Tomek was able to dig into the ground with his feet just enough to scoot himself forward. The only problem being that moving forward did nothing for him other than pushing his already burnt body into the glowing embers of the fire pit. However, he knew that timing would be the key to his escape, and with one more, large push, the right side of his body edged up onto the white, softball-sized rocks that encircled the pit.

The wooden chair tilted on the edge of the rocks, and he controlled the plane of his chest carefully with his legs. The heat radiating from the coals was almost unbearable, but he remained close to it while it singed his skin from below.

Tomek fought back the pain, lowered his rope-covered ribcage into the hot bed, and watched as the two-inch-thick, dry, twine rope caught fire and began to thin. Strand by strand separated and curled back in a flickering of red flame, giving way to the next set that followed suit. Tomek knew the rope was close to being completely burnt free as his lungs expanded fully for the first time.

He quickly retreated, gasping for air at that moment as his lungs filled with hot smoke from the fire. The internal fire war raged in his lungs as he rolled away from the chair and fell into the fire. He was free from the rope and the chair, even though the hair on the side of his head had been scorched off and his lungs had paid the ultimate price.

Coughing and gasping for air, his throat had been seared from the dryness of the heat it had been subjected to, but he was able to finally catch some semblance of a breath and got up to his knees.

He took a mental inventory of the items left in his pockets and knew he was knifeless. Even with a knife, Tony and Garran most likely wouldn't have thought much of it, since his wrists were cuffed tightly behind his back. However, his hands being secured behind his back was of very little concern to Tomek.

Lying on his back, he lifted his legs to the sky and worked his hands up behind his butt and over his legs until they cleared his boots. Thanks to a lifetime of Uncle's guided, stretching techniques and calisthenics, Tomek quickly had his hands in front of his body, where they rested comfortably.

Bending down, Tomek hurried as he untied and removed the lace on his right boot. Again, being raised by a military survival instructor meant that his boots were laced with 550 paracord. With the black lace free from the boot, he quickly fashioned large slipknots on each end. Sliding the slipknots over each foot, after routing it through the gap between the plastic and his skin, Tomek began to kick his legs back in forth in opposite strokes.

Pain radiated though his body with each kick of his blood-soaked sock.

The knife wound, courtesy of Garran that had gored the twin's foot, remained open and bleeding.

Tomek again rolled to his back and kicked his legs to the sky as if he was pedaling an upside down bike. As he fought through the pain, the friction generated by the cord biting into the cuffs made quick work of the weakened plastic. Having cut enough away, Tomek snapped his hands apart and was free. He then rolled to his stomach, where he stood up and kept the vast majority of his weight on his remaining good foot.

Tomek looked up to see the fire above him still illuminating the land at the top of the Ascension steps. Looking through the cabin, Tomek was disappointed that not a single, useful weapon remained. No gun or knives were present. Looking in the small room where the safe was located, he pulled random items from the shelves to the ground in an attempt to find something, anything that would help him protect himself.

Opening a purple, fishing tackle box, he thumbed through the contents and normally would have been quite satisfied with the gear inside. They had not spent a lot of time fishing on the lake inside the bowl, but it was at one time something he looked forward to doing. Tomek grabbed a spool of braided fishing line and looked at the package.

Fourteen pound test should do the trick, he thought in his head.

Tomek's next stop for a weapons check was the helicopter behind the cabin, which had landed in the clear part of the area where he and Drake had planned to put their garden.

Circling around the machine, it might as well have been an alien spacecraft as Tomek certainly had never been this close to any sort of aircraft before, let alone one of this caliber. After a few failed attempts at grasping the handles and locks incorrectly, Tomek opened the same rear sliding door they had watched Archer be pushed out of. Hopping inside, he looked around, seeing nothing but first aid kits in the storage bays. He grabbed the kits and tossed them out on the grass to be gone through later, as he knew that his facial burns would need antibiotic cream to ward off the infection he would be facing in the weeks ahead.

Tomek hopped out and went to the back of the helicopter, where he opened the fuel port to see if there was any way he could drain the gas to be used for fuel at a later date or at least prevent it from flying away a survivor. Reaching down into his pockets, he remembered the various items he had in his possession and knew that if given enough time he would be able find a multitude of things on the chopper that could be repurposed as weapons. Time was not a luxury he had as he heard movement in the grass behind him, thanks to the ill-timed snap of a twig.

Tomek hobbled around in the dark and heard a clear, unfamiliar voice say, "Back the fuck away from the helicopter."

22 CLAW

Tomek did not hesitate as he lunged towards the shadow of a man. Knowing it was not Tony, and with Drake being most likely dead, the only foe that remained to his knowledge was Ricardo.

Their bodies slammed together, falling to the ground. Tomek separated himself from the man as he rolled a few extra feet and got back up onto his feet as quickly as his injuries allowed.

Ricardo did the same and removed a six-inch knife from a sheath on his belt. Unarmed, Tomek's first instinct was to run, but he knew that in his current condition there was no way that his attempt to escape the man would be anything other than a comedy of errors.

Standing looking at each other, it was clear to Tomek that the man was as weak as himself. The fire light glowing from above mixed with the convenience of a full moon's shine protruding through the billowing smoke clouds allowed both Ricardo and Tomek to size each other up. Only, to Ricardo, this was a battle he had already lost. He had no idea Drake and Tomek were different people.

"You again, huh?" Ricardo asked as he swiped his knife at Tomek's abdomen, cutting nothing but air. "Looks like you had a rough time since last we danced."

"Last we danced?" Tomek replied, confused.

"Hell of a fire you started up there, boy," Ricardo said through a slurring of words, his lips and mouth unable to hold in the saliva that flooded from them. The snake venom had begun to take effect, and his face was swollen into a plethora of purplish, yellow lumps.

It was at that moment Tomek realized two very important things. Due to the puffy disfiguration of Ricardo's snake-fanged face, he could not see out of his left eye. Tomek would concentrate his attacks to that side, taking advantage of his opponent's weakness. The second important thing Tomek now knew was, thanks to Ricardo not knowing he and Drake were twins, he had confirmation that Drake was, in fact, alive.

Knowing that Ricardo was the last person to see Drake alive and had just confirmed so, an excited, rage-fueled energy surged through Tomek's body. The pain in Tomek's shish-kabobbed foot was completely absent as Tomek charged again at Ricardo, this time utilizing the blindness of the man's left eye to his advantage.

Tomek's strike landed square on the high cheekbone and squished into the swollen face. The venom-filled face absorbed the blow and shook like a bowl of gelatin. Ricardo's body spun and fell to the ground, and the knife-wielding man was unconscious before he hit the ground. Tomek had scored a one-punch knockout.

Tomek gained his composure, limped over to Ricardo, and stood looking down on him. Suddenly, Tomek's foot slipped and slid out from underneath him. Catching himself without falling, he looked down to see a large pool of blood on the ground.

What the hell? He thought to himself as he pulled Ricardo's shoulder, rolling the body over.

The knife Ricardo had tried to attack Tomek with just seconds earlier was buried deep into the man's gut, just below the last rib. Ricardo's eyes opened and locked with those of Tomek.

"Finish it," Ricardo whispered, but Tomek was unable to hear him over the sound of trees falling above them due to the fire.

"What?" Tomek asked.

Ricardo gestured for Tomek to come closer with his two fingers. Tomek granted the dying man's wish and leaned his ear down to Ricardo's mouth to ascertain Ricardo's last words.

Ricardo struggled to speak, and Tomek encouraged him. "Say what you need to say."

No more words came from Ricardo's mouth as his head fell back to the ground, silent. Tomek moved to stand up as Ricardo's hand grasped the back of the boy's neck, pulling it down. Ricardo slammed his teeth into Tomek's right ear and clenched down with the bite of a Nile crocodile dragging a gazelle into the river.

Tomek screamed, falling down to the ground beside Ricardo who spat out the entire top lobe of Tomek's severed ear. Reaching up, Tomek felt the warm blood pulsate from the wound. Tomek leaned on his right side, expecting to see Ricardo, but only a pool of blood remained.

Again, he struggled to get on his feet, but he knew that Ricardo would not make it far with the knife wound to his stomach. Letting the man who had just ruthlessly eaten a chunk of his face run away and die from attrition was not going to happen. Even in the dark of the flame-backed moonlight, the blood trail would be one of the easiest of his life.

Following the trail, he thought of Sypris, the best, damn tracking dog that ever existed. Thoughts of Sypris led his mind to Old Man Hawkins and of course, Uncle himself. Tomek tried to stay focused on the blood that was splattered every three feet on the ground along the side of the garden, but his mind drifted to the realization that this island would have been the perfect place for them all to live together in peace.

Peace, Tomek thought. He scoffed at the idea that mankind had any idea of what peace actually meant. If they did, he had certainly never seen it in his young life.

Patch by patch of blood, Tomek followed on the heels of Ricardo as he remained impressed at the distance and speed with which his prey was moving in relation to the amount of blood the man had already lost. As Tomek reached the massive, bottom door to the steps, he found blood smeared across the handle.

Looking up the steps, he located Ricardo halfway up the climb, on his knees. The knife was no longer in the belly of the man. It had been removed and now was held firmly against his neck by Drake, who was one step above him.

Drake's free hand held Ricardo's head back with a handful of hair. Ricardo's blood loss had drained him to the point of being unable to fight back. Ricardo slumped, with blood still bucketing out of his open stomach and chest wounds. His body weight would have tumbled down the steps had Drake let go of his grip on the man's hair.

Tomek walked up the steps slowly, gently placing his own damaged foot on each step as he ascended.

Ricardo looked up and struggled to talk just as he had before, but this time did manage to formulate an intelligible word.

"Twins."

"You want the honors?" Drake asked Tomek.

Tomek did not say a word as he replaced Drake's hand on the last remaining Stratton brother's head with his own. Tomek grabbed the thin, leather-bound necklace around his neck and yanked it free. Spinning it around his hand, the strap got shorter with each revolution until Tomek felt the thud.

Tomek pulled back on Ricardo's head, exposing his throat, and then, in one deep, spiteful motion, carved directly through the man's trachea with the lion's claw that adorned the bottom of his leather necklace. Ricardo gurgled as the claw sheared though the soft neck tissue.

The little remaining blood that was left in Ricardo's body poured out and down his chest as Tomek let go of his head and watched the lifeless corpse tumble down the black, rock steps, impacting the door at the bottom with a thud hard enough to kill even a healthy man.

The brothers looked at each other, and both smiled. Though they were not normally the type of guys to resort to hugging, they quickly found each other in a tight embrace.

"Man, your face is all kinds of fucked up," said Drake.

"Yep, at least everyone will be able to tell us apart," Tomek replied.

"It's an improvement, really," added Drake.

"Considering we were identical, I'll take that as a compliment," Tomek said with a smirk. "That's one hell of a barbecue you have going up there."

"Yea, about that…"

"What happened?"

Drake's excuse was as ridiculous as it was true. "I saw a snake."

Tomek threw his arm over his brother's shoulder to help secure his footing. "Well, then I guess we will have to garden and fish since you done burned the hell out of all the meat we could have hunted."

"Are they all dead?" Drake asked.

"Not yet. One left. A kid, like us. He saved my ass earlier but then knocked me out. It's a long story," said Tomek.

"Where is he now?" Drake asked.

Tomek didn't know the exact location of Tony right that moment, but as they got two steps from the bottom of the staircase, it was blatantly clear to the twins as they heard the helicopter's motor fire up and trigger the blades to begin their pre-flight rotation.

23 TRIAD

As Tomek and Drake rushed to the back side of the cabin, where the helicopter was, they saw Tony inside the fuselage, slamming shut the rear sliding door. Drake ran to the edge of the prop wash and shielded his eyes as the rotors lifted the skids from the ground before he could reach them.

The flashing, red and green, emergency beacons on the bottom of the helicopter's body lit up the darkness of the landing area as Tony gingerly gained altitude. Taking off in the dark would be a challenge with the nearby pines and the undulating topography of the island's bowl.

Tomek limped up to Drake, joining him under the aircraft as they both looked up and helplessly watched Tony make his ambitious escape.

"Just a kid like us, huh?" Drake asked, shrugging his shoulders.

Tomek did not verbally answer, but Drake felt uneasy as he saw a smile break across his twin's face. Drake wanted them all dead. Every single intruder to their island needed to never leave. If they really wanted to live their secluded life, then they had to truly be just that, secluded.

With enough altitude accumulated, Tony tilted the nose of the aircraft down with his controls, smoothly floating forward and over the pines.

"You know he will bring people back, and this will all happen again," Drake yelled, shaking his head.

Tomek seemed unfazed by the prospect of fighting another war on his new, island home and chillingly replied with the same big smile. "Just wait."

As soon as the words had left Tomek's mouth, an explosion vastly larger than anything the two of them had experience before ripped through the helicopter. The tail and its rotor separated from the body of the chopper in a massive fireball that ignited the top of the pines as it came crashing down, bringing every branch it encountered with it.

The cockpit remained somewhat still intact to the middle section as it spun wildly to the south, quickly losing altitude. The blades pierced the evening air with a whining screech as they lost their lift-generating, rotating syncopation.

Time seemed to slow down as Drake watched the chopper's remains fall, spinning not unlike a maple seed leaving the tree thanks to a late summer wind. Fire engulfed the interior as the rotors gave way, snapping in half and causing the fuselage to then fully plummet out of its uncontrolled spin.

Turning upside down, the small, glass windshield that protected Tony blew out in a massive burst of fire upon impact with the ground. The smell of burning rubber, leather, and jet fuel filled the air as both Drake and Tomek looked upon the crash site in awe.

"How did you know?" Drake asked his brother.

"I didn't have much down here to work with, but I did have some fishing line and a grenade," Tomek answered.

Drake looked at his brother, puzzled. "Where in the hell did you find a grenade?"

"I took it off the vest of the big guy with the axes."

"Was that the same one who cut down the bridge?" Drake asked.

Tomek smiled again through the pain of his damaged face. "Yup."

The two of them began walking towards the cabin to survey the damage of the cockpit's final landing site as Tomek added, "Yea, I had it in my pocket the whole time. The dumb shits never searched me."

"You gave them the opportunity to search you?"

"I was tied up two times, stabbed, burnt, hit, cut, and bit. I was fully tortured, actually. All while you were up there trying to burn snakes, so don't give me any shit," Tomek said, defending himself.

Drake yawned, "Whatever." He then stretched his arms over his head with an even larger yawn, asking, "Now what?"

"I need you to take a look at my foot, it is going to need to be stitched up," Tomek said.

Drake shook his head. "No way, man. That's going to need to be cauterized."

"You are not getting anywhere near my body with fire right now," said Tomek. "I think stiches and some antibiotic cream will do just fine."

"We don't have those kinds of supplies," Drake reminded him.

"Sure do. Took about four or five different med kits off the helicopter when I was tying the grenade on the landing rail."

"Where are they?" Drake asked.

Tomek motioned over behind them to their left. "Back behind that metal rail on the side of the garden. That's where I anchored the spool of fishing line."

This time it was Drake that was smiling. "You took down a helicopter with a grenade and some fishing line. Unreal, man. Unreal."

"Hey, I knew it would work, dammit. It was fourteen pound test, after all," Tomek said, laughing.

His brother's response again made him shrug his shoulders while shaking his head. "Well, you just have an answer for everything, don't you?"

24 MORNING

As the sun rose over the east edge of the lake-bowl, rock-wall ledge, Tomek sat in the small cabin's living room. Admiring the stitching on his foot, courtesy of Drake, he winced as his feet hit the cold floor. With all that had happened to them in just a few short days on the island, their time in Pine Run seemed like years ago. Drake heard Tomek rustling and hopping around as he exited from the back bedroom.

"I love the smell of charred remains in the morning," Drake joked, referencing their late-night activity of adding Garran, Ricardo, and Greggor's bodies to the blaze that had already contained Tony. Their final resting place would be the same as the helicopter's final, crash landing spot on a large patch of sand near the lake.

"How's the foot?" he asked, knowing that his suture skills were in need of improvement.

Tomek held his foot up to show Drake his work of art. "Looks like a laced up hockey skate, but it will do."

Drake agreed. "Throw a thick sock on, and let's take a look around. By the way, if you are worried about how your foot looks, don't look in the mirror."

Tomek knew that the branding on his face would eventually scar over and was not worried in regards to his vanity at all. Aside from the pain in his foot slowing him down, Tomek was eager to take the suggestion of his twin and go for a post-fire exploration of their island. From what they could tell, the fire on the upper island had burned all night, although the wind had died down at some point.

The helicopter's fire was at first intense, with the jet fuel making for a quick, crematory process. Once most of it had been consumed, only the fire retardant seat cushions and body of the aircraft remained as a charred, skeletal reminder of the insanity that had ensued the night before.

Stepping out onto the porch, they watched as a few trout fed on the early morning bugs that skidded across the glass-like water. Looking around, they shuffled through the remaining gear bags on the porch. Guns, ammo, axes, a few very nice knives, and fresh razor broadhead tipped arrows rounded out their newfound weapons cache, thanks to the Barr and Stratton families. Other than weapons, the hunters also provided enough MREs to last the twins almost a full year.

Both twins geared up, loading their newfound shotguns, along with a few favored pistols. There would be a time that they would return to life with the simplicity of bows and arrows, but for now, they were unsure of what to expect after climbing the steps.

The steps were daunting for Tomek as he labored up each one slowly and in pain. Grimacing with each step, he was relieved as they opened the top door. Tomek plopped himself down on a small patch of unburnt grass to give his foot a rest as Drake pushed the heavy, stairwell door closed, securing it behind him.

Both of the twins were pleasantly surprised at the condition of the fire-swept island. From their vantage point, it was clear to see that, while the meadow grasslands had been destroyed, the blaze was unable to survive in the swampland without the aid of the strong winds. The fern valley remained hidden by the large, unfazed section of hardwood. A few mature trees showed signs of heat stress, with wilted leaves up their sides, edging the swamp, but otherwise, they remained standing. The twins felt confident each limb would return to life in the following spring.

"Where to?" Drake asked, helping Tomek up to his feet.

Tomek didn't answer him. He just began to walk slowly, attempting not to put pressure on his injured foot. Drake followed behind Tomek as he headed west towards the one tree on the rock ledge that had survived the meadow's fire. It took longer than he had expected to traverse over the charcoaled ground that had been burnt down to the dirt, but standing at the tree somehow felt like an accomplishment of sorts.

The waves crashed into the jagged rocks below, where just days before Tomek had run the gauntlet against a lion and won.

"You know, if you don't turn around and look at the scorch behind us, this really is a beautiful place," said Drake, taking in the moment of tranquility.

Tomek turned around and leaned against the tree, using it as a crutch and taking in a deep breath. "It's all beautiful," he replied, centering his spine on the trunk of the tree.

The tree had survived the fire and now stood as a visual marker for that side of the island. The lone tree was almost poetic in nature. Out of the ashes, growth will arise in the shadow of this survivor.

However, as strong as the tree appeared to be, the fire had taken an unseen toll. The weakened roots lurched forward, snapping under Tomek's minuscule body weight, and the tree quickly began its descent over the island's edge and down to the deadly rocks below. The top-heavy lumber pulled the roots up and out of the ground with a whiplash-like effect, throwing Tomek from the trunk. As Tomek began to stumble towards the edge, off balance, out of control, and unable to use his hurt foot, he looked at Drake in panic.

Drake saw the fear in his brother's eyes and sprinted towards him. As slow as a tree that size would take to grow, ripping from the earth and falling in devastation spanned only mere seconds. These seconds were all that Ascension Island needed to claim Tomek's soul, fittingly vanquishing him in the same manner it did the lion.

Drake's hands grasped Tomek's coat. The gripping motion caused Tomek's forward momentum to spin, resulting in this right arm being stripped out of the jacket as his body continued toward the edge. Drake held the empty sleeve of the denim coat and pulled with all his might backwards in a jerking motion as he fell to the ground.

Tomek's left arm had remained tight in the jacket, and Drake's forceful yank had stopped the island's intentions of killing his twin, bringing him back onto solid land, where he landed on his stomach. Tomek's face was flat against the soot-laden path. Pushing himself up, he looked at Drake and got to his feet.

Tomek looked around, and Drake noticed the panic in his brother's eyes had been replaced with an intense focus. Tomek stepped forward to the edge, looking out over the blue waters of Lake Michigan below him, and triumphantly yelled, while beating a closed fist upon his chest, "This is my island. This is my prison. This is my home. I will protect it. I am the snake, not the mouse."

The End

Thank you for reading the original trilogy of the Twins of Prey series.

Twins of Prey 4 – Lockdown is COMING SOON!

I hope my Uncle is proud.

W.C. Hoffman

Praying For War

Did you enjoy the *Twins of Prey* series?

Then you will love *Praying for War.*

The first book in,

The Collin War Chronicles.

https://wchoffman.weebly.com/my-book-store.html

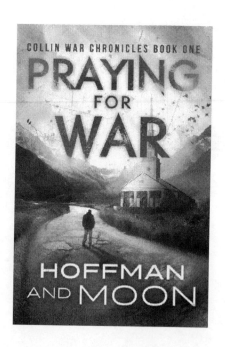

Special Thanks

The Following Kickstarter backers helped make this dream of mine come true. I am forever thankful for your support.

Greg & Linda Hathaway

Michael & Deedra Barr

Jeff & Brook Stratton

Tim Moon

Brett & Amy Routhier

J. Robert Quillen

Thomas Zilling

John Frewin

Derek Freeman

Andreas Gustafsson

John Justin Green

Michael Chrome

Jonathan Scharff II

Traditional Archer Bob Young

Chad Bowden

Matthew Akers

Kevin White

Made in the USA
Columbia, SC
22 February 2023

12833473R00100